The landscape [was] what it should [be.] One moment h[e...] place, returning [... foray] against the Mexicans. Mexicans! Travis caught at that identification. . . . Mexicans . . . And he was an Apache, one of the Eagle people. . . . No!

He was not of the past. He was Travis Fox, of the very late twentieth century, not a nomad of the middle nineteenth! He was of Team A of the project!

Then he saw it:

The wreckage crumpled on the mountain side was identifiable—a spaceship! Cold fear gripped him and his own head went back; from between his tight lips came a cry as desolate and despairing as the one the animals had voiced.

Stranded in space, how could he free his people from their own past—and from those who planned to use it for their own bitter ends?

THE DEFIANT AGENTS

THE DEFIANT AGENTS

ANDRE NORTON

SF
ace books
A Division of Charter Communications Inc.
A GROSSET & DUNLAP COMPANY
51 Madison Avenue
New York, New York 10010

THE DEFIANT AGENTS

An ACE Book

Cover art by Davis Meltzer

Sixth Ace printing: July 1978
Seventh Ace printing: September 1980

8 0 9
Manufactured in the United States of America

FOR P. SCHUYLER MILLER

who expressed a wish for some Apache colonists,

and CHARLES F. KELLEY

who has a liking for "time agent" tales.

I

No WINDOWS broke any of the four plain walls of the office; there was no focus of outer-world sunlight on the desk there. Yet the five disks set out on its surface appeared to glow—perhaps the heat of the mischief they could cause . . . had caused . . . blazed in them.

But fanciful imaginings did not cushion or veil cold, hard fact. Dr. Gordon Ashe, one of the four men peering unhappily at the display, shook his head slightly as if to free his mind of such cobwebs.

His neighbor to the right, Colonel Kelgarries, leaned forward to ask harshly: "No chance of a mistake?"

"You saw the detector." The thin gray string of a man behind the desk answered with chill precision. "No, no possible mistake. These five have definitely been snooped."

"And two choices among them," Ashe murmured. That was the important point now.

"I thought these were under maximum security," Kelgarries challenged the gray man.

Florian Waldour's remote expression did not

change. "Every possible precaution was in force. There was a sleeper—a hidden agent—planted—"

"Who?" Kelgarries demanded.

Ashe glanced around at his three companions—Kelgarries, colonel in command of one sector of Project Star, Florian Waldour, the security head on the station, Dr. James Ruthven . . .

"Camdon!" he said, hardly able to believe this answer to which logic had led him.

Waldour nodded.

For the first time since he had known and worked with Kelgarries Ashe saw him display open astonishment.

"Camdon? But he was sent us by—" The colonel's eyes narrowed. "He must have been sent. . . . There were too many cross checks to fake that!"

"Oh, he was sent, all right." For the first time there was a note of emotion in Waldour's voice. "He was a sleeper, a very deep sleeper. They must have planted him a full twenty-five or thirty years ago. He's been just what he claimed to be as long as that."

"Well, he certainly was worth their time and trouble, wasn't he?" James Ruthven's voice was a growling rumble. He sucked in thick lips, continuing to stare at the disks. "How long ago were these snooped?"

Ashe's thoughts turned swiftly from the enormity of the betrayal to that important point. The time element—that was the primary concern now that the damage was done, and they knew it.

"That's one thing we don't know." Waldour's reply came slowly as if he hated the admission.

"We'll be safer, then, if we presume the very earliest period." Ruthven's statement was as ruthless in its implications as the shock they had had when Waldour announced the disaster.

"Eighteen months ago?" Ashe protested.

But Ruthven was nodding. "Camdon was in on this from the very first. We've had the tapes in and out for study all that time, and the new detector against snooping was not put in service until two weeks ago. This case came up on the first checking round, didn't it?" he asked Waldour.

"First check," the security man agreed. "Camdon left the base six days ago. But he has been in and out on his liaison duties from the first."

"He had to go through those search points every time," Kelgarries protested. "Thought nothing could get through those." The colonel brightened. "Maybe he got his snooper films and then couldn't take them off base. Have his quarters been turned out?"

Waldour's lips lifted in a grimace of exasperation. "Please, Colonel," he said wearily, "this is not a kindergarten exercise. In confirmation of his success, listen . . ." He touched a button on his desk and out of the air came the emotionless chant of a newscaster.

"Fears for the safety of Lassiter Camdon, space expeditor for the Western Conference Space Council, have been confirmed by the discovery of burned wreckage in the mountains. Mr. Camdon was returning from a mission to the Star Laboratory when his plane lost contact with Ranger Field. Reports of a storm in that vicinity immediately raised concern—" Waldour snapped off the voice.

"True—or a cover for his escape?" Kelgarries wondered aloud.

"Could be either. They may have deliberately written him off when they had all they wanted," Waldour acknowledged. "But to get back to our troubles—Dr. Ruthven is right to assume the worst. I believe we can only insure the recovery of our project by thinking that these tapes were snooped anywhere from eighteen months ago to last week. And we must work accordingly!"

There was silence in the room as they all considered that. Ashe slipped down in his chair, his thoughts enmeshed in memories. First there had been Operation Retrograde, when specially trained "time agents" had shuttled back and forth in history, striving to locate and track down the mysterious source of alien knowledge which the eastern Communistic nations had suddenly begun to use.

Ashe himself and a younger partner, Ross Murdock, had been part of the final action which had solved the mystery, having traced that source of knowledge not to an earlier and forgotten Terran civilization but to wrecked spaceships from an eon-old galactic empire—an empire which had flourished when glacial ice covered most of Europe and northern America and Terrans were cave-dwelling primitives. Murdock, trapped by the Reds in one of those wrecked ships, had inadvertently summoned its original owners, who had descended to trace—through the Russian time stations—the looters of their wrecks, destroying the whole Red time-travel system.

But the aliens had not chanced on the parallel

4

western system. And a year later that had been put into Project Folsom One. Again Ashe, Murdock, and a newcomer, the Apache Travis Fox, had gone back into time to the Arizona of the Folsom hunters, discovering what they wanted—two ships, one wrecked, the other intact. And when the full efforts of the project had been centered on bringing the intact ship back into the present, chance had triggered controls set by the dead alien commander. A party of four, Ashe, Murdock, Fox and a technician, had then made an involuntary voyage into space, touching three worlds on which the galactic civilization of the far past was now marked only by ruins.

Voyage tape fed into the controls of the ship had taken the men, and, when rewound, had—by a miracle—returned them to Terra with a cargo of similar tapes found in a building on a world which might have been the central capital for a government comprised not of countries or of worlds but of solar systems. Tapes—each one the key to another planet.

And that ancient galactic knowledge was treasure such as the Terrans had never dreamed of possessing, though there were the attendant fears that such discoveries could be weapons in enemy hands. There had been an enforced sharing with other nations of tapes chosen at random at a great drawing. And each nation secretly remained convinced that, in spite of the untold riches it might hold as a result of chance, its rivals had done better. Right at this moment, Ashe did not in the least doubt, there were agents of his own party intent on accomplishing at the Red project just what Camdon had done there.

However, that did not help in solving their present dilemma concerning Operation Cochise, one part of their project, but perhaps the most important now.

Some of the tapes were duds, either too damaged to be useful, or set for worlds hostile to Terrans lacking the equipment the earlier star-traveling race had had at its command. Of the five tapes they now knew had been snooped, three would be useless to the enemy.

But one of the remaining two . . . Ashe frowned. One was the goal toward which they had been working feverishly for a full twelve months. To plant a colony across the gulf of space—a successful colony—later to be used as a stepping-stone to other worlds . . .

"So we have to move faster." Ruthven's comment reached Ashe through his stream of memories.

"I thought you required at least three more months to conclude personnel training," Waldour observed.

Ruthven lifted a fat hand, running the nail of a broad thumb back and forth across his lower lip in a habitual gesture Ashe had learned to mistrust. As the latter stiffened, bracing for a battle of wills, he saw Kelgarries come alert too. At least the colonel more often than not was ready to counter Ruthven's demands.

"We test and we test," said the fat man. "Always we test. We move like turtles when it would be better to race like greyhounds. There is such a thing as overcaution, as I have said from the first. One would think"—his accusing glance included Ashe and Kelgarries—"that there had never been any improvising in the project, that all had always been done by the book. I say that this is the time we must take the big gamble, or else we may find we have been outbid for space entirely. Let those others discover even one alien installation they can master and—" his thumb shifted from his lip, grinding down on the desk top as if it were crushing some venturesome but entirely unimportant insect—"and we are finished before we really begin."

There were a number of men in the project who would agree with that, Ashe knew. And a greater number in the country and conference at large. The public was used to reckless gambles which paid off, and there had been enough of those in the past to give an impressive argument for that point of view. But Ashe, himself, could not agree to a speed-up. He had been out among the stars, shaved disaster too closely because the proper training had not been given.

"I shall report that I advise a take-off within a week," Ruthven was continuing. "To the council I shall say that—"

"And I do not agree!" Ashe cut in. He glanced at Kelgarries for the quick backing he expected, but instead there was a lengthening moment of silence. Then the colonel spread out his hands and said sullenly:

"I don't agree either, but I don't have the final say so. Ashe, what would be needed to speed up any take-off?"

It was Ruthven who replied. "We can use the Redax, as I have said from the start."

Ashe straightened, his mouth tight, his eyes hard and angry.

"And I'll protest that . . . to the council! Man, we're dealing with human beings—selected volunteers, men who trust us—not with laboratory animals!"

Ruthven's thick lips pouted into what was close to a smile of derision. "Always the sentimentalists, you experts in the past! Tell me, Dr. Ashe, were you always so thoughtful of your men when you sent agents back into time? And certainly a voyage into space is less a risk than time travel. These volunteers know what they have signed for. They will be ready—"

"Then you propose telling them about the use of Redax—what it does to a man's mind?" countered Ashe.

"Certainly. They will receive all necessary instructions."

Ashe was not satisfied and he would have spoken again, but Kelgarries interrupted:

"If it comes to that, none of us here has any right to make final decisions. Waldour has already sent in his report about the snoop. We'll have to await orders from the council."

Ruthven levered himself out of his chair, his solid bulk stretching his uniform coveralls. "That is correct, Colonel. In the meantime I would suggest we all check to see what can be done to speed up each one's position of labor." Without another word, he tramped to the door.

Waldour eyed the other two with mounting impatience. It was plain he had work to do and wanted them to leave. But Ashe was reluctant. He had a feeling that matters were slipping out of his control, that he was about to face a crisis which was somehow worse than just a major security leak. Was the enemy always on the other side of the world? Or could he wear the same uniform, even share the same goals?

In the outer corridor he still hesitated, and Kelgarries, a step or so in advance, looked back over his shoulder impatiently.

"There's no use fighting—our hands are tied." His words were slurred, almost as if he wanted to disown them.

"Then you'll agree to use the Redax?" For the second time within the hour Ashe felt as if he had taken a step only to have firm earth turn into slippery, shifting sand underfoot.

"It isn't a matter of my agreeing. It may be a matter of getting through or not getting through—now. If they've had eighteen months, or even twelve . . . !" The colonel's fingers balled into a fist. "And *they* won't be delayed by any humanitarian reasoning—"

"Then you believe Ruthven will win the council's approval?"

"When you are dealing with frightened men, you're talking to ears closed to anything but what they want to hear. After all, we can't prove that the Redax will be harmful."

"But we've only used it under rigidly controlled conditions. To speed up the process would mean a total disregard of those controls. Snapping a party of men and women back into their racial past and holding them there for too long a period . . ." Ashe shook his head.

"You have been in Operation Retrograde from the start, and we've been remarkably successful—"

"Operating in a different way, educating picked

men to return to certain points in history where their particular temperaments and characteristics fitted the roles they were selected to play, yes. And even then we had our percentage of failures. But to try this—returning people not physically into time, but *mentally and emotionally* into prototypes of their ancestors—that's something else again. The Apaches have volunteered, and they've been passed by the psychologists and the testers. But they're Americans of today, not tribal nomads of two or three hundred years ago. If you break down some barriers, you might just end up breaking them all."

Kelgarries was scowling. "You mean—they might revert utterly, have no contact with the present at all?"

"That's just what I do mean. Education and training, yes, but full awakening of racial memories, no. The two branches of conditioning should go slowly and hand in hand, otherwise—real trouble!"

"Only we no longer have the time to go slow. I'm certain Ruthven will be able to push this through—with Waldour's report to back him."

"Then we'll have to warn Fox and the rest. They must be given a choice in the matter."

"Ruthven said that would be done." The colonel did not sound convinced of that.

Ashe snorted. "If I hear him telling them, I'll believe it!"

"I wonder whether we can. . . ."

Ashe half turned and frowned at the colonel. "What do you mean?"

"You said yourself that we had our failures in time travel. We expected those, accepted them, even when they hurt. When we asked for volunteers for this project we had to make them understand that there was a heavy element of risk involved. Three teams of recruits—the Eskimos from Point Barren, the Apaches, and the Islanders—all picked because their people had a high survival rating in the past, to be colonists on widely different types of planets. Well, the Eskimos and the Islanders aren't matched to any of the worlds on those snooped tapes, but Topaz is waiting for the Apaches. And we may have to move them in there in a hurry. It's a rotten gamble any way you see it!''

"I'll appeal directly to the council."

Kelgarries shrugged. "All right. You have my backing."

But you believe such an effort hopeless?''

"You know the red-tape merchants. You'll have to move fast if you want to beat Ruthven. He's probably on a straight line now to Stanton, Reese, and Margate. This is what he has been waiting for!''

"There are the news syndicates; public opinion would back us—''

"You don't mean that, of course." Kelgarries was suddenly coldly remote.

Ashe flushed under the heavy brown which overlay his regular features. To threaten a silence break was near blasphemy here. He ran both hands down the fabric covering his thighs as if to rub away some soil on his palms.

"No," he replied heavily, his voice dull. "I guess I don't. I'll contact Hough and hope for the best."

"Meanwhile," Kelgarries spoke briskly, "we'll do what we can to speed up the program as it now stands. I suggest you take off for New York within the hour—''

"Me? Why?" Ashe asked with a trace of suspicion.

"Because I can't leave without acting directly against orders, and that would put us wrong immediately. You see Hough and talk to him personally—put it to him straight. He'll have to have all the facts if he's going to counter any move from Stanton before the council. You know every argument we can use and all the proof on our side, and you're authority enough to make it count."

"If I can do all that, I will." Ashe was alert and eager. The colonel, seeing his change of expression, felt easier.

But Kelgarries stood a moment watching Ashe as he hurried down a side corridor, before he moved on slowly to his own box of office. Once inside he sat for a long unhappy time staring at the wall and seeing nothing but the pictures produced by his thoughts. Then he pressed a button and read off the symbols which flashed on a small visa-screen set in his desk. Another button pushed, and he picked up a hand mike to relay an order which might postpone trouble for a while. Ashe was far too valuable a man to lose, and his emotions could boil him straight into disaster over this.

"Bidwell—reschedule Team A. They are to go to the Hypno-Lab instead of the reserve in ten minutes."

Releasing the mike, he again stared at the wall. No one dared interrupt a hypno-training period, and this one would last three hours. Ashe could not possibly see the trainees before he left for New York. And that would remove one temptation from his path—he would not talk at the wrong time.

Kelgarries' mouth twisted sourly. He had no pride in what he was doing. And he was perfectly certain that Ruthven would win and that Ashe's fears of Redax were well founded. It all came back to the old basic tenet of the service: the end justified the means. They must use every method and man under their control to make sure that Topaz would remain a western possession, even though that strange planet now swung far beyond the sky which covered both the western and eastern alliances on Terra. Time had run out too fast; they were being forced to play what cards they held, even though those might be very low ones. Ashe would be back, but not, Kelgarries hoped, until this had been decided one way or another. Not until this was finished.

Finished! Kelgarries blinked at the wall. Perhaps *they* were finished, too. No one would know until the transport ship landed on that other world which appeared on the direction tape symbolized by a jewel-like disk of gold-brown which had given it the code name of Topaz.

II

THERE WERE an even dozen of the air-born guardians,
each following the swing of its own orbital path just
within the atmospheric envelope of the planet which
glowed as a great bronze-golden gem in the four-
world system of a yellow star. The globes had been
launched to form a web of protection around Topaz
six months earlier, and the highest skill had gone into
their production. Just as contact mines sown in a
harbor could close that landfall to ships not knowing
the secret channel, so was this world supposedly
closed to any spaceship not equipped with the signal
to ward off the sphere missiles.

That was the theory of the new off-world settlers
whose protection they were to be, already tested as
well as possible, but as yet not put to the ultimate
proof. The small bright globes spun undisturbed
across a two-mooned sky at night and made reassur-
ing blips on an installation screen by day.

Then a thirteenth object winked into being, began
the encircling, closing spiral of descent. A sphere
resembling the warden-globes, it was a hundred
times their size, and its orbit was purposefully con-

trolled by instruments under the eye and hand of a human pilot.

Four men were strapped down on cushioned slingseats in the control cabin of the Western Alliance ship, two hanging where their fingers might reach buttons and levers, the others merely passengers, their own labor waiting for the time when they would set down on the alien soil of Topaz. The planet hung there in their visa-screen, richly beautiful in its amber gold, growing larger, nearer, so that they could pick out features of seas, continents, mountain ranges, which had been studied on tape until they were familiar, yet now were strangely unfamiliar too.

One of the warden-globes alerted, oscillated in its set path, whirled faster as its delicate interior mechanisms responded to the awakening spark which would send it on its mission of destruction. A relay clicked, but for the smallest fraction of a millimeter failed to set the proper course. On the instrument, far below, which checked the globe's new course the mistake was not noted.

The screen of the ship spiraling toward Topaz registered a path which would bring it into violent contact with the globe. They were still some hundreds of miles apart when the alarm rang. The pilot's hand clawed out at the bank of controls; under the almost intolerable pressure of their descent, there was so little he could do. His crooked fingers fell back powerlessly from the buttons and levers; his mouth was a twisted grimace of bleak acceptance as the beat of the signal increased.

One of the passengers forced his head around on the padded rest, fought to form words, to speak to his companion. The other was staring ahead at the screen, his thick lips wide and flat against his teeth in a snarl of rage.

"They . . . are . . . here. . . ."

Ruthven paid no attention to the obvious as stated by his fellow scientist. His fury was a red, pulsing thing inside him, fed by his own helplessness. To be pinned here so near his goal, fastened up as a target for an inanimate but cunningly fashioned weapon, ate into him like a stream of deadly acid. His big gamble would puff out in a blast of fire to light up Topaz's sky, with nothing left—nothing. On the armrest of his sling-seat his nails scratched deep.

The four men in the control cabin could only sit and watch, waiting for the rendezvous which would blot them out. Ruthven's flaming anger was a futile blaze. His companion in the passenger seat had closed his eyes, his lips moving soundlessly in an expression of his own scattered thoughts. The pilot and his assistant divided their attention between the screen, with its appalling message, and the controls they could not effectively use, feverishly seeking a way out in these last moments.

Below them in the bowl of the ship were those who would not know the end consciously—save in one compartment. In a padded cage a prick-eared head stirred where it rested on forepaws, slitted eyes blinked, aware not only of familiar surroundings, but also of the tension and fear generated by human minds and emotions levels above. A pointed nose raised, and there was a growling deep in a throat covered with thick buff-gray hair.

The growl aroused another similar captive. Knowing yellow eyes met yellow eyes. An intelligence, which was certainly not that of the animal body which contained it, fought down instinct raging to send both those bodies hurtling at the fastenings of the twin cages. Curiosity and the ability to adapt had been bred into both from time immemorial. Then something else had been added to sly and cunning brains. A step up had been taken—to weld intelligence to cunning, connect thought to instinct.

More than a generation earlier mankind had chosen barren desert—the "white sands" of New Mexico—as a testing ground for atomic experiments. Humankind could be barred, warded out of the radiation limits; the natural desert dwellers, four-footed and winged, could not be so controlled.

For thousands of years, since the first southward roving Amerindian tribes had met with their kind, there had been a hunter of the open country, a smaller cousin of the wolf, whose natural abilities had made an undeniable impression on the human mind. He was in countless Indian legends as the Shaper or the Trickster, sometimes friend, sometimes enemy. Godling for some tribes, father of all evil for others. In the wealth of tales the coyote, above all other animals, had a firm place.

Driven by the press of civilization into the badlands and deserts, fought with poison, gun, and trap, the coyote had survived, adapting to new ways with all his legendary cunning. Those who had reviled him as vermin had unwillingly added to the folklore which surrounded him, telling their own tales of robbed traps, skillful escapes. He continued to be a trickster, laughing on moonlit nights from the tops of ridges at those who would hunt him down.

Then, close to the end of the twentieth century,

when myths were scoffed at, the stories of the coyote's slyness began once more on a fantastic scale. And finally scientists were sufficiently intrigued to seek out this creature that seemed to display in truth all the abilities credited to his immortal namesake by pre-Columbian tribes.

What they discovered was indeed shattering to certain closed minds. For the coyote had not only adapted to the country of the white sands; he had evolved into something which could not be dismissed as an animal, clever and cunning, but limited to beast range. Six cubs had been brought back on the first expedition, coyote in body, their developing minds different. The grandchildren of those cubs were now in the ship's cages, their mutated senses alert, ready for the slightest chance of escape. Sent to Topaz as eyes and ears for less keenly endowed humans, they were not completely under the domination of man. The range of their mental powers was still uncomprehended by those who had bred, trained, and worked with them from the days their eyes had opened and they had taken their first wobbly steps away from their dams.

The male growled again, his lips wrinkling back in a snarl as the emanations of fear from the men he could not see reached panic peak. He still crouched, belly flat, on the protecting pads of his cage; but he strove now to wriggle closer to the door, just as his mate made the same effort.

Between the animals and those in the control cabin lay the other—forty of them. Their bodies were cushioned and protected with every ingenious device known to those who had placed them there so many weeks earlier. Their minds were free of the ship, roving into places where men had not trod before, a territory potentially more dangerous than any solid earth could ever be.

Operation Retrograde had returned men bodily into the past, sending agents to hunt mammoths, follow the roads of the Bronze Age traders, ride with Attila and Genghis Khan, pull bows among the archers of ancient Egypt. But Redax returned men in mind to the paths of their ancestors, or this was the theory. And those who slept here and now in their narrow boxes, lay under its government, while the men who had arbitrarily set them so could only assume they were actually reliving the lives of Apache nomads in the wide southwestern wastes of the late eighteenth and early nineteenth centuries.

Above, the pilot's hand pushed out again, fighting the pressure to reach one particular button. That, too, had been a last-minute addition, an experiment which had only had partial testing. To use it was the final move he could make, and he was already half convinced of its uselessness.

With no faith and only a very wan hope, he sent that round of metal flush with the board. What followed no one ever lived to explain.

On the planet the installation which tracked the missiles flashed on a screen bright enough to blind momentarily the duty man on watch, and its tracker was shaken off course. When it jiggled back into line it was no longer the efficient eye-in-the-sky it had been, though its tenders were not to realize that for an important minute or two.

While the ship, now out of control, sped in dizzy whirls toward Topaz, engines fought blindly to stabilize, to re-establish their functions. Some succeeded, some wobbled in and out of the danger zone, two failed. And in the control cabin three dead men spun in prisoning seats.

Dr. James Ruthven, blood bubbling from his lips with every shallow breath he could draw, fought the stealthy tide of blackness which crept up his brain, his stubborn will holding to rags of consciousness, refusing to acknowledge the pain of his fatally injured body.

The orbiting ship was on an erratic path. Slowly the machines were correcting, relays clicking, striving to bring it to a landing under auto-pilot. All the ingenuity built into a mechanical brain was now centered in landing the globe.

It was not a good landing, in fact a very bad one, for the sphere touched a mountain side, scraped down rocks, shearing away a portion of its outer bulk. But the mountain barrier was now between it and the base from which the missiles had been launched, and the crash had not been recorded on that tracking instrument. So far as the watchers several hundred miles away knew, the warden in the sky had performed as promised. Their first line of defense had proven satisfactory, and there had been no unauthorized landing on Topaz.

In the wreckage of the control cabin Ruthven pawed at the fastenings of his sling-chair. He no longer tried to suppress the moans every effort tore out of him. Time held the whip, drove him. He rolled from his seat to the floor, lay there gasping as again he fought doggedly to remain above the waves— those frightening, fast-coming waves of dark faintness.

Somehow he was crawling, crawling along a tilted

surface until he gained the well where the ladder to the lower section hung, now at an acute angle. It was that angle which helped him to the next level.

He was too dazed to realize the meaning of the crumpled bulkheads. There was a spur of bare rock under his hands as he edged over and around twisted metal. The moans were now a gobbling, burbling, almost continuous cry as he reached his goal—a small cabin still intact.

For long moments of anguish he paused by the chair there, afraid that he could not make the last effort, raise his almost inert bulk up to the point where he could reach the Redax release. For a second of unusual clarity he wondered if there was any reason for this supreme ordeal, whether any of the sleepers could be aroused. This might now be a ship of the dead.

His right hand, his arm, and finally his bulk over the seat, he braced himself and brought his left hand up. He could not use any of the fingers; it was like lifting numb, heavy weights. But he lurched forward, swept the unfeeling lump of cold flesh down against the release in a gesture which he knew must be his final move. And, as he fell back to the floor, Dr. Ruthven could not be certain whether he had succeeded or failed. He tried to screw his head around, to focus his eyes upward at that switch. Was it down or still stubbornly up, locking the sleepers into confinement? But there was a fog between; he could not see it—or anything.

The light in the cabin flickered, was gone as another circuit in the broken ship failed. It was dark, too, in the small cubby below which housed the two cages. Chance, which had snuffed out nineteen lives in the space globe, had missed ripping open that cabin on the mountain side. Five yards down the corridor the outside fabric of the ship was split wide open, the crisp air native to Topaz entering, sending a message to two keen noses through the combination of odors now pervading the wreckage.

And the male coyote went into action. Days ago he had managed to work loose the lower end of the mesh which fronted his cage, but his mind had told him that a sortie inside the ship was valueless. The odd rapport he'd had with the human brains, unknown to them, had operated to keep him to the old role of cunning deception, which in the past had saved countless of his species from sudden and violent death. Now with teeth and paws he went diligently to work, urged on by the whines of his mate, that tantalizing smell of an outside world tickling their nostrils—a wild world, lacking the taint of man-places.

He slipped under the loosened mesh and stood up to paw at the front of the female's cage. One forepaw caught in the latch and pressed it down, and the weight of the door swung against him. Together they were free now to reach the corridor and see ahead the subdued light of a strange moon beckoning them on into the open.

The female, always more cautious than her mate, lingered behind as he trotted forward, his ears a-prick with curiosity. Their training had been the same since cubhood—to range and explore, but always in the company and at the order of man. This was not according to the pattern she knew, and she was suspicious. But to her sensitive nose the smell of the ship was an offense, and the puffs of breeze from without enticing. Her mate had already slipped through the break; now he barked with excitement and wonder, and she trotted on to join him.

Above, the Redax, which had never been intended to stand rough usage, proved to be a better survivor of the crash than most of the other installations. Power purred along a network of lines, activated beams, turned off and on a series of fixtures in those coffin-beds. For five of the sleepers—nothing. The cabin which had held them was a flattened smear against the mountain side. Three more half aroused, choked, fought for life and breath in a darkness which was a mercifully short nightmare, and succumbed.

But in the cabin nearest the rent through which the coyotes had escaped, a young man sat up abruptly, looking into the dark with wide-open, terror-haunted eyes. He clawed for purchase against the smooth edge of the box in which he had laid, somehow got to his knees, weaving weakly back and forth, and half fell, half pushed to the floor where he could stand only by keeping his hold on the box.

His flailing hand rapped painfully against an upright surface which his questing fingers identified hazily as an exit. Unconsciously he fumbled along the surface of the door until it gave under that weak pressure. Then he was out, his head swimming, drawn by the light behind the wall rent.

He progressed toward that in a scrambling crawl, making his way over the splintered skin of the globe. Then he dropped with a jarring thud onto the mound of earth the ship had pushed before it during its downward slide. Limply he tumbled on in a small cascade of clods and sand, hitting against a less movable rock with force enough to roll him over on his back and stun him again.

The second and smaller moon of Topaz swung brightly through the sky, its weird green rays making the blood-streaked face of the explorer an alien mask. It had passed well on to the horizon, and its large yellow companion had risen when a yapping broke the small sounds of the night.

As the *yipp, yipp, yipp* arose in a crescendo, the man stirred, putting one hand to his head. His eyes opened, he looked vaguely about him and sat up. Behind him was the torn and ripped ship, but he did not look back at it.

Instead, he got to his feet and staggered out into the direct path of the moonlight. Inside his brain there was a whirl of thoughts, memories, emotions. Perhaps Ruthven or one of his assistants could have explained that chaotic mixture for what it was. But for all practical purposes Travis Fox—Amerindian Time Agent, member of Team A, Operation Cochise—was far less of a thinking animal now than the two coyotes paying their ritual addresses to a moon which was not the one of their vanished homeland.

Travis wavered on, drawn somehow by that howling. It was familiar, a thread of something real through all the broken clutter in his head. He stumbled, fell, crawled up again, but he kept on.

Above, the female coyote lowered her head, drew a test sniff of a new scent. She recognized that as part of the proper way of life. She yapped once at her mate, but he was absorbed in his night song, his muzzle pointed moonward as he voiced a fine wailing.

Travis tripped, pitched forward on his hands and knees, and felt the jar of such a landing shoot up his stiffened forearms. He tried to get up, but his body only twisted, so he landed on his back and lay looking up at the moon.

A strong, familiar odor . . . then a shadow looming above him. Hot breath against his cheek, and the swift sweep of an animal tongue on his face. He flung up his hand, gripped thick fur, and held on as if he had found one anchor of sanity in a world gone completely mad.

III

TRAVIS, one knee braced against the red earth, blinked as he parted a screen of tall rust-brown grass with cautious fingers to look out into a valley where golden mist clouded most of the landscape. His head ached with dull persistence, the pain fostered in some way by his own bewilderment. To study the land ahead was like trying to see through one picture interposed over another and far different one. He knew what ought to be there, but what was before him was very dissimilar.

A buff-gray shape flitted through the tall cover grass, and Travis tensed. *Mba'a*—coyote? Or were these companions of his actually *ga-n*, spirits who could choose their shape at will and had, oddly, this time assumed the bodies of man's tricky enemy? Were they *ndendai*—enemies—or *dalaanbiyat'i*, allies? In this mad world he did not know.

Ei'dik'e? His mind formed a word he did not speak: Friend?

Yellow eyes met his directly. Dimly he had been aware, ever since awaking in this strange wilderness with the coming of morning light, that the four-footed ones trotting with him as he walked aimlessly had unbeastlike traits. Not only did they face him eye-to-eye, but in some ways they appeared able to read his thoughts.

He had longed for water to ease the burning in his throat, the ever-present pain in his head, and the creatures had nudged him in another direction, bringing him to a pool where he had mouthed liquid with a strange sweet, but not unpleasant taste.

Now he had given them names, names which had come out of the welter of dreams which shadowed his stumbling journey across the weird country.

Nalik'ideyu (Maiden-Who-Walks-Ridges) was the female who continued to shepherd him along, never venturing too far from his side. Naginlta (He-Who-Scouts-Ahead) was the male who did just that, disappearing at long intervals and then returning to face the man and his mate as if conveying some report necessary to their journey.

It was Nalik'ideyu who sought out Travis now, her red tongue lolling from her mouth as she panted. Not from exertion, he was certain of that. No, she was excited and eager . . . on the hunt! That was it—a hunt!

Travis' own tongue ran across his lips as an impression hit him with feral force. There was meat —rich, fresh—just ahead. Meat that lived, waiting to be killed. Inside him his own avid hunger roused, shaking him farther out of the crusting dream.

His hands went to his waist, but the groping fingers did not find what vague memory told him should be there—a belt, heavy with knife in sheath.

He examined his own body with attention to find he was adequately covered by breeches of a smooth, dull brown material which blended well with the vegetation about him. He wore a loose shirt, belted in at the narrow waist by a folded strip of cloth, the ends of which fluttered free. On his feet were tall moccasins, the leg pieces extending some distance up his calves, the toes turned up in rounded points.

Some of this he found familiar, but these were fragments of memory; again his mind fitted one picture above another. One thing he did know for sure—he had no weapons. And that realization struck home with a thrust of real and terrible fear which tore away more of the bewilderment cloaking his mind.

Nalik'ideyu was impatient. Having advanced a step or two, she now looked back at him over her shoulder, yellow eyes slitted, her demand on him as instant and real as if she had voiced understandable words. Meat was waiting, and she was hungry. Also she expected Travis to aid in the hunt—at once.

Though he could not match her fluid grace in moving through the grass, Travis followed her, keeping to cover. He shook his head vigorously, in spite of the stab of pain the motion cost him, and paid more attention to his surroundings. It was apparent that the earth under him, the grass around, the valley of the golden haze, were all real, not part of a dream. Therefore that other countryside which he kept seeing in a ghostly fashion was a hallucination.

Even the air which he drew into his lungs and expelled again, had a strange smell, or was it taste? He could not be sure which. He knew that hypnotraining could produce queer side effects, but . . . this . . .

Travis paused, staring unseeingly before him at

the grass still waving from the coyote's passage.
Hypno-training! What was that? Now three pictures
fought to focus in his mind: the two landscapes
which did not match and a shadowy third. He shook
his head again, his hands to his temples. This—this
only was real: the ground, the grass, the valley, the
hunger in him, the hunt waiting . . .

He forced himself to concentrate on the immediate
present and the portion of world he could see, feel,
scent, which lay here and now about him.

The grass grew shorter as he proceeded in
Nalik'ideyu's wake. But the haze was not thinning.
It seemed to hang in patches, and when he ventured
through the edge of a patch it was like creeping
through a fog of golden, dancing motes with here
and there a glittering speck whirling and darting like
a living thing. Masked by the stuff, Travis reached a
line of brush and sniffed.

It was a warm scent, a heavy odor he could not
identify and yet one he associated with a living
creature. Flat to earth, he pushed head and shoulders
under the low limbs of the bush to look ahead.

Here was a space where the fog did not hold, a
pocket of earth clear under the morning sun. And
grazing there were three animals. Again shock
cleared a portion of Travis' bemused brain.

They were about the size, he thought, of an-
telopes, and they had a general resemblance to those
beasts in that they had four slender legs, a rounded
body, and a head. But they had alien features, so
alien as to hold him in open-mouthed amazement.

The bodies had bare spots here and there, and
patches of creamy—fur? Or was it hair which hung
in strips, as if the creatures had been partially

plucked in a careless fashion? The necks were long and moved about in a serpentine motion, as though their spines were as limber as reptiles'. On the end of those long and twisting necks were heads which also appeared more suitable to another species—broad, rather flat, with a singular toadlike look—but furnished with horns, set halfway down the nose, horns which began in a single root and then branched into two sharp points.

They were unearthly! Again Travis blinked, brought his hand up to his head as he continued to view the browsers. There were three of them: two larger and with horns, the other a smaller beast with less of the ragged fur and only the beginning button of a protuberance on the nose; it was probably a calf.

One of those mental alerts from the coyotes broke his absorption. Nalik'ideyu was not interested in the odd appearance of the grazing creatures; she was intent upon their usefulness in another way—as a full and satisfying meal—and she was again impatient with him for his dull response.

His examination took a more practical turn. An antelope's defense was speed, though it could be tricked into hunting range through its inordinate curiosity. The slender legs of these beasts suggested a like degree of speed, and Travis had no weapons at all.

Those nose horns had an ugly look; this thing might be a fighter rather than a runner. But the suggestion which had flashed from coyote to him had taken root. Travis was hungry, he was a hunter, and here was meat on the hoof, queer as it looked.

Again he received a message. Naginlta was on the opposite side of the clearing. If the creatures depended on speed, then Travis believed they could probably outrun not only him but the coyotes as well—which left cunning and some sort of plan.

Travis glanced at the cover where he knew Nalik'ideyu crouched and from which had come that flash of agreement. He shivered. These were truly no animals, but *ga-n, ga-n* of power! And as *ga-n* he must treat them, accede to their will. Spurred by that, the Apache gave only flicks of attention to the browsers while at the same time he studied the part of the landscape uncovered by mist.

Without weapons or speed, they must conceive a trap. Again Travis sensed that agreement which was *ga-n* magic, and with it the strong impression urging him to the right. He was making progress with skill he did not even recognize and which he had never been conscious of learning.

The bushes and small, droop-limbed trees, their branches not clothed with leaves from proper twigs but with a reddish bristly growth protruding directly from their surfaces, made a partial wall for the pocket-sized meadow. That screen reached a rocky cleft where the mist curled in a long tongue through a wall twice Travis' height. If the browsers could be maneuvered into taking the path through that cleft . . .

Travis searched about him, and his hands closed upon the oldest weapon of his species, a stone pulled from an earth pocket and balanced neatly in the palm of his hand. It was a long chance but his best one.

The Apache took the first step on a new and fearsome road. These *ga-n* had put their thoughts—or their desires—into his mind. Could he so contact them in return?

With the stone clenched in his fist, his shoulders back against the wall not too far from the cleft opening, Travis strove to think out, clearly and simply, this poor plan of his. He did not know that he was reacting the way scientists deep space away had hoped he might. Nor did Travis guess that at this point he had already traveled far beyond the expectations of the men who had bred and trained the two mutant coyotes. He only believed that this might be the one way he could obey the wishes of the two spirits he thought far more powerful than any man. So he pictured in his mind the cleft, the running creatures, and the part the *ga-n* could play if they so willed.

Assent—in its way as loud and clear as if shouted. The man fingered the stone, weighed it. There would probably be just one moment when he could use it to effect, and he must be ready.

From this point he could no longer see the small meadow where the grazers were. But Travis knew, as well as if he watched the scene, that the coyotes were creeping in, belly flat to earth, adding a feline stealth and patience to their own cunning.

There! Travis' head jerked, the alert had come, the drive was beginning. He tensed, gripping his stone.

A yapping bark was answered by a sound he could not describe, a noise which was neither cough nor grunt but a combination of both. Again a yap-yap . . .

A toad-head burst through the screen of brush, the double horn on its nose festooned with a length of grass torn up by the roots. Wide eyes—milky and seeming to be without pupils—fastened on Travis, but he could not be sure the thing saw him, for it kept on, picking up speed as it approached the cleft. Behind it ran the calf, and that guttural cry was bubbling from its broad flat lips.

The long neck of the adult writhed, the frog-head swung closer to the ground so that the twin points of the horn were at a slant—aimed now at Travis. He had been right in his guess at their deadliness, but he had only a fleeting chance to recognize that fact as the thing bore down, its whole attitude expressing the firm intention of goring him.

He hurled his stone and then flung his body to one side, stumbling and rolling into the brush where he fought madly to regain his feet, expecting at any moment to feel trampling hoofs and thrusting horns. There was a crash to his right, and the bushes and grass were wildly shaken.

On his hands and knees the Apache retreated, his head turned to watch behind him. He saw the flirt of a triangular flap-tail in the mouth of the cleft. The calf had escaped. And now the threshing in the bushes stilled.

Was the thing stalking him? He got to his feet, for the first time hearing clearly the continued yapping, as if a battle was in progress. Then the second of the adult beasts came into view, backing and turning, trying to keep lowered head with menacing double horn always pointed to the coyotes dancing a teasing, worrying circle about it.

One of the coyotes flung up its head, looked upslope, and barked. Then, as one, both rushed the fighting beast, but for the first time from the same side, leaving it a clear path to retreat. It made a rush before which they fled easily, and then it whirled with a speed and grace, which did not fit its ungainly, ill-proportioned body, and jumped toward the cleft, the coyotes making no effort to hinder its escape.

Travis came out of cover, approaching the brush which had concealed the crash of the other animal. The actions of the coyotes had convinced him that there was no danger now; they would never have allowed the escape of their prey had the first beast not been in difficulties.

His shot with the stone, the Apache decided as he stood moments later surveying the twitching crumpled body, must have hit the thing in the head, stunning it. Then the momentum of its charge had carried it full force against the rock to kill it. Blind luck—or the power of the *ga-n?* He pulled back as the coyotes came padding up shoulder to shoulder to inspect the kill. It was truly more theirs than his.

Their prey yielded not only food but a weapon for Travis. Instead of the belt knife he had remembered having, he was now equipped with two. The double horn had been easy to free from the shattered skull, and some careful work with stones had broken off one prong at just the angle he wanted. So now he had a short and a longer tool, defense. At least they were better than the stone with which he had entered the hunt.

Nalik'ideyu pushed past him to lap daintily at the water. Then she sat up on her haunches, watching Travis as he smoothed the horn with a stone.

"A knife," he said to her, "this will be a knife. And—" he glanced up, measuring the value of the wood represented by trees and bushes— "then a bow. With a bow we shall hunt better."

The coyote yawned, her yellow eyes half closed, her whole pose one of satisfaction and contentment.

"A knife," Travis repeated, "and a bow." He needed weapons; he had to have them!

Why? His hand stopped scraping. Why? The toad-faced double horn had been quick to attack, but Travis could have avoided it, and it had not hunted him first. Why was he ridden by this fear that he must not be unarmed?

He dipped his hand into the pool of the spring and lifted the water to cool his sweating face. The coyote moved, turned around in the grass, crushing down the growth into a nest in which she curled up, head on paws. But Travis sat back on his heels, his now idle hands hanging down between his knees, and forced himself to the task of sorting out jumbled memories.

This landscape was wrong—totally unlike what it should be—but it was real. He had helped kill this alien creature. He had eaten its meat, raw. Its horn lay within touch now. All that was real and un-changeable. Which meant that the rest of it, that other desert world in which he had wandered with his kind, ridden horses, raided invading men of an-other race, that was not real—or else far, far re-moved from where he now sat.

Yet there had been no dividing line between those two worlds. One moment he had been in the desert place, returning from a successful foray against the Mexicans. Mexicans! Travis caught at the identifica-tion, tried to use it as a thread to draw closer to the beginning of his mystery.

Mexicans . . . And he was an Apache, one of the Eagle people, one who rode with Cochise. No!

Sweat again beaded his face where the water had cooled it. He was not of that past. He was Travis Fox, of the very late twentieth century, not a nomad of the middle nineteenth! He was of Team A of the project!

The Arizona desert and then this! From one to the other in an instant. He looked about him in rising fear. Wait! He had been in the dark when he got out of the desert, lying in a box. Getting out, he had crawled down a passage to reach moonlight, strange moonlight.

A box in which he had lain, a passage with smooth metallic walls, and an alien world at the end of it.

The coyote's ears twitched, her head came up, she was staring at the man's drawn face, at his eyes with their core of fear. She whined.

Travis caught up two pieces of horn, thrust them into his sash belt, and got to his feet. Nalik'ideyu sat up, her head cocked a little to one side. As the man turned to seek his own back trail she padded along in his wake and whined for Naginlta. But Travis was more intent now on what he must prove to himself than he was on the actions of the two animals.

It was a wandering trail, and now he did not question his skill in being able to follow it so unerringly. The sun was hot. Winged things buzzed from the bushes, small scuttling things fled from him through the tall grass. Once Naginlta growled a warning which led them all to a detour, and Travis might not have picked up the proper trace again had not the coyote scout led him to it.

"Who are you?" he asked once, and then guessed it would have better been said, "What are you?" These were not animals, or rather they were more than the animals he had always known. And one part of him, the part which remembered the desert rancherias where Cochise had ruled, said they were spirits. Yet that other part of him . . . Travis shook his head, accepting them now for what they were—welcome company in an alien place.

The day wore on close to sunset, and still Travis followed that wandering trail. The need which drove him kept him going through the rough country of hills and ravines. Now the mist lifted above towering walls of mountains very near him, yet not the mountains of his memory. These were dull brown, with a forbidding look, like sun-dried skulls baring teeth in warning against all comers.

With great difficulty, Travis topped a rise. Ahead against the skyline stood both coyotes. And, as the man joined them, first one and then the other flung back its head and sounded the sobbing, shattering cry which had been a part of that other life.

The Apache looked down. His puzzle was answered in part. The wreckage crumpled on the mountain side was identifiable—a spaceship! Cold fear gripped him and his own head went back; from between his tight lips came a cry as desolate and despairing as the one the animals had voiced.

IV

FIRE, mankind's oldest ally, weapon, tool, leaped high before the naked stone of the mountain side. Men sat cross-legged about it, fifteen of them. And behind, guarded by the flames and that somber circle, were the women. There was a uniformity in this gathering. The members were plainly all of the same racial stock, of medium height, stocky yet fined down to the peak of stamina and endurance, their skin brown, their shoulder-length hair black. And they were all young—none over thirty, some still in their late teens. Alike, too, was a certain drawn look in their faces, a tenseness of the eyes and mouth as they listened to Travis.

"So we must be on Topaz. Do any of you remember boarding the ship?"

"No. Only that we awoke within it." Across the fire one chin lifted; the eyes which caught Travis' held a deep, smoldering anger. "This is more trickery of the Pinda-lick-o-yi, the White Eyes. Between us there has never been fair dealing. They have broken their promise as a man breaks a rotten stick, for their words are as rotten. And it was you, Fox, who brought us to listen to them."

A stir about the circle, a murmur from the women.

"And do I not also sit here with you in this strange wilderness?" he countered.

"I do not understand," another of the men held out his hand, palm up, in a gesture of asking—"what has happened to us. We were in the old Apache world . . . I, Jil-Lee, was riding with Cuchillo Negro as we went down to the taking of Ramos. And then I was here, in a broken ship and beside me a dead man who was once my brother. How did I come out of the past of our people into another world across the stars?"

"Pinda-lick-o-yi tricks!" The first speaker spat into the fire.

"It was the Redax, I think," Travis replied. "I heard Dr. Ashe discuss this. A new machine which could make a man remember not his own past, but the past of his ancestors. While we were on that ship we must have been under its influence, so we lived as our people lived a hundred years or more ago—"

"And the purpose of such a thing?" Jil-Lee asked.

"To make us more like our ancestors perhaps. It is part of what they told us at the project. To venture into these new worlds requires a different type of man than lives on Terra today. Traits we have forgotten are needed to face the dangers of wild places."

"You, Fox, have been beyond the stars before, and you found there were such dangers to face?"

"It is true. You have heard of the three worlds I saw when the ship from the old days took us off, unwilling, to the stars. Did you not all volunteer to pioneer in this manner so you could also see strange and new things?"

"But we did not agree to be returned to the past in medicine dreams and be sent unknowingly into space!"

Travis nodded. "Deklay is right. But I know no more than you why we were so sent, or why the ship crashed. We have found Dr. Ruthven's body in the cabin with that new installation. Only we have discovered nothing else which tells us why we were brought here. With the ship broken, we must stay."

They were silent now, men and women alike. Behind them lay several days of activity, nights of exhausted slumber. Against the cliff wall lay the packs of supplies they had salvaged from the wreck. By mutual consent they had left the vicinity of the broken globe, following their old custom of speedily withdrawing from a place of death.

"This is a world empty of men?" Jil-Lee wanted to know.

"So far we have found only animal signs, and the *ga-n* have not warned us of anything else—"

"Those devil ones!" Again Deklay spat into the fire. "I say we should have no dealings with them. The *mba'a* is no friend to the People."

Again a murmur which seemed one of agreement answered that outburst. Travis stiffened. Just how much influence had the Redax had over them? He knew from his own experience that sometimes he had an odd double reaction—two different feelings which almost sickened him when they struck simultaneously. And he was beginning to suspect that with some of the others the return to the past had been far more deep and lasting. Now Jil-Lee was actually to reason out what had happened. While Deklay had

reverted to an ancestor who had ridden with Victorio
or Magnus Colorado! Travis had a flash of premoni-
tion, a chill which made him half foresee a time
when the past and the present might well split them
apart—fatally.

"Devil or *ga-n*." A man with a quiet face, rather
deeply sunken eyes, spoke for the first time. "We
are in two minds because of this Redax, so let us not
do anything in haste. Back in the desert world of the
People I have seen the *mba'a*, and he was very
clever. With the badger he went hunting, and when
the badger had dug up the rat's nest, so did the *mba'a*
wait on the other side of the thorny bush and catch
those who would escape that way. Between him and
the badger there was no war. These two who sit over
yonder now—they are also hunters and they seem
friendly to us. In a strange place a man needs all the
help he can find. Let us not call names out of old
tales, which may mean nothing in fact."

"Buck speaks straightly," Jil-Lee agreed. "We
seek a camp which can be defended. For perhaps
there are men here whose hunting territory we have
invaded, though we have not yet seen them. We are a
people small in number and alone. Let us walk softly
on trails which are strange to our feet."

Inwardly Travis sighed in relief. Buck, Jil-Lee
. . . for the moment their sensible words appeared
to swing the opinions of the party. If either of them
could be established as *haldzil*, or clan leader, they
would all be safer. He himself had no aspirations in
that direction and dared not push too hard. It had
been his initial urging which had brought them as
volunteers into the project. Now he was doubly

suspect, and especially by those who thought as Deklay, he was considered too alien to their old ways.

So far their protests had been fewer than he anticipated. Although brothers and sisters had followed each other into the team after the immemorial desire of Apaches to cling to family ties, they were not a true clan with solidity of that to back them, but representatives of half a dozen.

Basically, back on Terra, they had all been among the most progressive of their people—progressive, that is, in the white man's sense of the word. Travis had a fleeting recognition of his now oblique way of thinking. He, too, had been marked by the Redax. They had all been educated in the modern fashion and all possessed a spirit of adventure which marked them over their fellows. They had volunteered for the team and successfully passed the tests to weed out the temperamentally unfit or faint-hearted. But all that was before Redax. . . .

Why had they been submitted to that? And why this flight? What had pushed Dr. Ashe and Murdock and Colonel Kelgarries, time agents he knew and trusted, into dispatching them without warning to Topaz? Something had happened, something which had given Dr. Ruthven ascendancy over those others and had started them on this wild trip.

Travis was conscious of a stir about the firelit circle. The men were rising, moving back into the shadows, stretching out on the blankets they had found among other stores on the ship. They had discovered weapons there—knives, bows, quivers of arrows, all of which they had been trained to use in the intensive schooling of the project and which needed no more repair than they themselves could give. And the rations they carried were field supplies, few of them. Tomorrow they must begin hunting in earnest. . . .

"Why has this thing been done to us?" Buck was beside Travis, those quiet eyes sliding past him to seek the fire once more. "I do not think you were told when the rest of us were not—"

Travis seized upon that. "There are those who say that I knew, agreed?"

"That is so. Once we stood at the same place in time—in our thoughts, our desires. Now we stand at many places, as if we climbed a stairway, each at his own speed—a stairway the Pinda-lick-o-yi has sent us upon. Some here, some there, some yet farther above . . ." He sketched a series of step outlines in the air. "And in this there is trouble—"

"The truth," Travis agreed. "Yet it is also true that I knew nothing of this, that I climb with you on these stairs."

"So I believe. But there comes a time when it is best not to be a woman stirring a pot of boiling stew but rather one who stands quietly at a distance—"

"You mean?" Travis pressed.

"I say that alone among us you have crossed the stars before, therefore new things are not so hard to understand. And we need a scout. Also the coyotes run in your footsteps, and you do not fear them."

It made good sense. Let him scout ahead of the party, taking the coyotes with him. Stay away from the camp for a while and speak small—until the people on Buck's stairway were more closely united.

"I go in the morning," Travis agreed. He could slip away tonight, but just now he could not force himself away from the fire, from the companionship.

"You might take Tsoay with you," Buck continued.

Travis waited for him to enlarge on that suggestion. Tsoay was one of the youngest of their group, Buck's own cross-cousin and near-brother.

"It is well," Buck explained, "that we learn this land, and it has always been our custom that the younger walk in the footprints of the older. Also, not only should trails be learned, but also men."

Travis caught the thought behind that. Perhaps by taking the younger men as scouts, one after another, he could build up among them a following of sorts. Among the Apaches, leadership was wholly a matter of personality. Until the reservation days, chieftains had gained their position by force of character alone, though they might come successively from one family clan over several generations.

He did not want the chieftainship here. No, but neither did he want growing whispers working about him to cut him off from his people. To every Apache severance from the clan was a little death. He must have those who would back him if Deklay, or those who thought like Deklay, turned grumbling into open hostility.

"Tsoay is one quick to learn," Travis agreed. "We go at dawn—"

"Along the mountain range?" Buck inquired.

"If we seek a protected place for the ranchería, yes. The mountains have always provided good strongholds for the People."

"And you think there is a need for a fort?"

Travis shrugged. "I have been one day's journey

out into this world. I saw nothing but animals. But that is no promise that elsewhere there are no enemies. The planet was on the tapes we brought back from that other world, and so it was known to the others who once rode between star and star as we rode between ranch and town. If they had this world set on a journey tape, it was for a reason; that reason may still be in force.''

"Yet it was long ago that these star people rode so. . . .'' Buck mused. "Would the reason last so long?''

Travis remembered two other worlds, one of weird desert inhabited by beast things—or had they once been human, human to the point of possessing intelligence?—that had come out of sand burrows at night to attack a spaceship. And the second world where the ruins of a giant city had stood choked with jungle vegetation, where he had made a blowgun from tubes of rustless metal as a weapon gift for small winged men—but were they men? Both had been remnants of that ancient galactic empire.

"Some things could so remain,'' he answered soberly. "If we find them, we must be careful. But first a good site for the rancheria.''

"There is no return to home for us,'' Buck stated flatly.

"Why do you say that? There could be a rescue ship later—''

The other raised his eyes again to Travis. "When you slept under the Redax how did you ride?''

"As a warrior—raiding . . . living . . .''

"And I—I was one with *go'ndi*,'' Buck returned simply.

"But—''

45

"But the white man had assured us that such power—the power of a chief—does not exist? Yes, the Pinda-lick-o-yi has told us so many things. He is busy, busy with his tools, his machines, always busy. And those who think in another fashion cannot be measured by his rules, so they are foolish dreamers. Not all white men think so. There was Dr. Ashe—he was beginning to understand a little.

"Perhaps I, too, am standing still, halfway up the stairway of the past. But of this I am very sure: For us, there will be no return to our own place. And the time will come when something new shall grow from the seed of the past. Also it is necessary that you be one of the tenders of that growth. So I urge you, take Tsoay, and the next time, Lupe. For the young who may be swayed this way and that by words—as the wind shakes a small tree—must be given firm roots."

In Travis education warred with instinct, just as the picture Redax had planted in his mind had warred with his awaking to this alien landscape. Yet now he believed he must be guided by what he felt. And he knew that no man of his race would claim *go'ndi*, the power of spirit known only to a great chief, unless he had actually felt it swell within him. It might have been fostered by hallucination in the past, but the aura of it carried into the here and now. And Travis had no doubts that Buck believed implicitly in what he said, and that belief carried credulity to others.

"This is wisdom, *Nantan*—"

Buck shook his head. "I am no *nantan*, no chief. But of some things I am sure. You also be sure of what lies within you, younger brother!"

On the third day, ranging eastward along the base

of the mountain range, Travis found what he believed would be an acceptable camp site. There was a canyon with a good spring of water cut round by well-marked game trails. A series of ledges brought him up to a small plateau where scrub wood could be used to build the wickiups. Water and food lay within reach, and the ledge approach was easy to defend. Even Deklay and his fellow malcontents were forced to concede the value of the site.

His duty to the clan accomplished, Travis returned to his own concern, one which had haunted him for days. Topaz had been taped by men of the vanished star empire. Therefore, the planet was important, but why? As yet he had found no indication that anything above the intelligence level of the split horns was native to this world. But he was gnawed by the certainty that there *was* something here, waiting. . . . And the desire to learn what it was became an ever-burning ache.

Perhaps he was what Deklay had accused him of being, one who had come to follow the road of the Pinda-lick-o-yi too closely. For Travis was content to scout with only the coyotes for company, and he did not find the loneliness of the unknown planet as intimidating as most of the others.

He was checking his small trail pack on the fourth day after they had settled on the plateau when Buck and Jil-Lee hunkered down beside him.

"You go to hunt—?" Buck broke the silence first. "Not for meat."

"What do you fear? That *ndendai*—enemy people—have marked this as their land?" Jil-Lee questioned.

"That may be true, but now I hunt for what this

world was at one time, the reason why the ancient star men marked it as their own."

"And this knowledge may be of value to us?" Jil-Lee asked slowly. "Will it bring food to our mouths, shelter for our bodies—mean life for us?"

"All that is possible. It is the unknowing which is bad."

"True. Unknowing is always bad," Buck agreed. "But the bow which is fitted to one hand and strength of arm, may not be suited to another. Remember that, younger brother. Also, do you go alone?"

"With Naginlta and Nalik'ideyu I am not alone."

"Take Tsoay with you also. The four-footed ones are indeed *ga-n* for the service of those they like, but it is not good that man walks alone from his kind."

There it was again, the feeling of clan solidarity which Travis did not always share. On the other hand, Tsoay would not be a hindrance. On other scouts the boy had proved to have a keen eye for the country and a liking for experimentation which was not a universal attribute even among those of his own age.

"I would go to find a path through the mountains; it may be a long trail," Travis half protested.

"You believe what you seek may lie to the north?"

Travis shrugged. "I do not know. How can I? But it will be another way of seeking."

"Tsoay shall go. He keeps silent before older warriors as is proper for the untried, but his thoughts fly free as do yours," Buck replied. "It is in him also, this need to see new places."

"There is this," Jil-Lee got to his feet, "—do not

go so far, brother, that you may not easily find a way to return. This is a wide land, and within it we are but a handful of men alone—''

''That, too, I know.'' Travis thought he could read more than one kind of warning in Jil-Lee's words.

They were the second day away from the plateau camp, and climbing, when they chanced upon the pass Travis had hoped might exist. Before them lay an abrupt descent to what appeared to be open plains country cloaked in a dusky amber Travis now knew was the thick grass found in the southern valleys. Tsoay pointed with his chin.

''Wide land—good for horses, cattle, ranches . . .''

But all those lay far beyond the black space surrounding them. Travis wondered if there was any native animal which could serve man in place of the horse.

''Do we go down?'' Tsoay asked.

From this point Travis could sight no break far out on the amber plain, no sign of any building or any disturbance of its smooth emptiness. Yet it drew him. ''We go,'' he decided.

Close as it had looked from the pass, the plain was yet a day and a night, spent in careful watching by turns, ahead of them. It was midmorning of the second day that they left the foothill breaks, and the grass of the open country was waist high about them. Travis could see it rippling where the coyotes threaded ahead. Then he was conscious of a persistent buzzing, a noise which irritated faintly until he was compelled to trace it to its source.

The grass had been trampled flat for an irregular patch, with a trail of broken stalks out of the heart of the plain. At one side was a buzzing, seething mass of glitter-winged insects which Travis already knew as carrion eaters. They arose reluctantly from their feast as he approached.

He drew a short breath which was close to a grunt of astounded recognition. What lay there was so impossible that he could not believe the evidence of his eyes. Tsoay gave a sharp exclamation, went down on one knee for a closer examination, then looked at Travis over his shoulder, his eyes wide, more than a trace of excitement in his voice.

"Horse dung—and fresh!"

V

"THERE WAS one horse, unshod but ridden. It came here from the plains and it had been ridden hard, going lame. There was a rest here, maybe shortly after dawn." Travis sorted out what they had learned by a careful examination of the ground.

Nalik'ideyu and Naginlta, Tsoay, watched and listened as if the coyotes as well as the boy could understand every word.

"There is that also—" Tsoay indicated the one trace left by the unknown rider, an impression blurred as if some attempt had been made to conceal it.

"Small and light, the rider is both. Also in fear, I think—"

"We follow?" Tsoay asked.

"We follow," Travis assented. He looked to the coyotes, and as he had learned to do, thought out his message. This trail was the one to be followed. When the rider was sighted they were to report back if the Apaches had not yet caught up.

There was no visible agreement; the coyotes simply vanished through the wall of grass.

"Then there are others here," Tsoay said as he

and Travis began their return to the foothills. ''Perhaps there was a second ship—''

''That horse,'' Travis said, shaking his head. ''There was no provision in the project for the shipping of horses.''

''Perhaps they have always been here.''

''Not so. To each world its own species of beasts. But we shall know the truth when we look upon that horse—and its rider.''

It was warmer this side of the mountains, and the heat of the plains beat at them. Travis thought that the horse might well be seeking water if allowed his head. Where did he come from? And why had his rider gone in haste and fear?

This was rough, broken country and the tired, limping horse seemed to have picked the easiest way through it, without any hindrance from the man with him. Travis spotted a soft patch of ground with a deep set impression. This time there had been no attempt at erasure; the boot track was plain. The rider had dismounted and was leading the horse—yet he was moving swiftly.

They followed the tracks around the bend of a shallow cut and found Nalik'ideyu waiting for them. Between her forefeet was a bundle still covered with smears of soft earth, and behind her were drag marks from a hole under the overhang of a bush. The coyote had plainly just disinterred her find. Travis squatted down to examine it, using his eyes before his hands.

It was a bag made of hide, probably the hide of one of the split horns by its color and the scraps of long hair which had been left in a simple decorative fringe along the bottom. The sides had been laced together neatly by someone used to working in leather, the closing flap lashed down tightly with braided thong loops.

As the Apache leaned closer to it he could smell a mixture of odors—the hide itself, horse, wood smoke, and other scents—strange to him. He undid the fastenings and pulled out the contents.

There was a shirt, with long full sleeves, of a gray wool undyed after the sheep. Then a very bulky short jacket which, after fingering it doubtfully, Travis decided was made of felt. It was elaborately decorated with highly colorful embroidery, and there was no mistaking the design—a heavy antlered Terran deer in mortal combat with what might be a puma. It was bordered with a geometric pattern of beautiful, oddly familiar work. Travis smoothed it flat over his knee and tried to remember where he had seen its like before. . . . a book! An illustration in a book! But which book, when? Not recently, and it was not a pattern known to his own people.

Twisted into the interior of the jacket was a silklike scarf, clear, light blue—the blue of Terra's cloudless skies on certain days, so different from the yellow shield now hanging above them. A small case of leather, with silhouetted designs cut from hide and affixed to it, designs as intricate and complex as the embroidery on the jacket—art of a high standard. In the case a knife and spoon, the bowl and blade of dull metal, the handles of horn carved with horse heads, the tiny wide open eyes set with glittering stones.

Personal possessions dear to the owner, so that when they must be abandoned for flight they were hidden with some hope of recovery. Travis slowly repacked them, trying to fold the garments into their original creases. He was still puzzled by those designs.

"Who?" Tsoay touched the edge of the jacket with one finger, his admiration for it plain to read.

"I don't know. But it is of our own world."

"That is a deer, though the horns are wrong," Tsoay agreed. "And the puma is very well done. The one who made this knows animals well."

Travis pushed the jacket back into the bag and laced it shut. But he did not return it to the hiding place. Instead, he made it a part of his own pack. If they did not succeed in running down the fugitive, he wanted an opportunity for closer study, a chance to remember just where he had seen that picture before.

The narrow valley where they had discovered the bag sloped upward, and there were signs that their quarry found the ground harder to cover. The second discard lay in open sight—again a leather bag which Nalik'ideyu sniffed and then began to lick eagerly, thrusting her nose into its flaccid interior.

Travis picked it up, finding it damp to the touch. It had an odd smell, like that of sour milk. He ran a finger around inside, brought it out wet; yet this was neither water bag nor canteen. And he was completely mystified when he turned it inside out, for though the innner surface was wet, the bag was empty. He offered it to the coyote, and she took it promptly.

Holding it firmly to the earth with her forepaws, she licked the surface, though Travis could see no deposit which might attract her. It was clear that that bag had once held some sort of food.

"Here they rested," Tsoay said. "Not too far ahead now—"

But now they were in the kind of country where a man could hide in order to check on his back trail. Travis studied the terrain and then made his own plans. They would leave the plainly marked trace of the fugitive, strike out upslope to the east and try to parallel the other's route. In that maze of rock outcrops and wood copses there was tricky going.

Nalik'ideyu gave a last lick to the bag as Travis signaled her. She regarded him, then turned her head to survey the country before them. At last she trotted on, her buff coat melting into the vegetation. With Naginlta she would scout the quarry and keep watch, leaving the men to take the longer way around.

Travis pulled off his shirt, folding it into a packet and tucking it beneath the folds of his sash-belt, just as his ancestors had always done before a fight. Then he cached his pack and Tsoay's. As they began the stiff climb they carried only their bows, the quivers slung on their shoulders, and the long-bladed knives. But they flitted like shadows and, like the coyotes, their red-brown bodies became indistinguishable against the bronze of the land.

They should be, Travis judged, not more than an hour away from sundown. And they had to locate the stranger before the dark closed in. His respect for their quarry had grown. The unknown might have been driven by fear, but he held to a good pace and headed intelligently for just the kind of country which would serve him best. If Travis could only remember where he had seen the like of that embroidery! It had a meaning which might be important now. . . .

Tsoay slipped behind a wind-gnarled tree and disappeared. Travis stooped under a line of bush limbs. Both were working their way south, using the peak ahead as an agreed landmark, pausing at intervals to examine the landscape for any hint of a man and horse.

Travis squirmed snake fashion into an opening between two rock pillars and lay there, the westerning sun hot on his bare shoulders and back, his chin propped on his forearm. In the band holding back his hair he had inserted some concealing tufts of wiry mountain grass, the ends of which drooped over his rugged features.

Only seconds earlier he had caught that fragmentary warning from one of the coyotes. What they sought was very close, it was right down there. Both animals were in ambush, awaiting orders. And what they found was familiar, another confirmation that the fugitive was Terran, not native to Topaz.

With searching eyes, Travis examined the site indicated by the coyotes. His respect for the stranger was raised another notch. In time either he or Tsoay might have sighted that hideaway without the aid of the animal scouts; on the other hand, they might have failed. For the fugitive had truly gone to earth, using some pocket or crevice in the mountain wall.

There was no sign of the horse, but a branch here and there had been pulled out of place, the scars of their removal readable when one knew where to look. Odd, Travis began to puzzle over what he saw. It was almost as if whatever pursuit the stranger feared would come not at ground level but from above; the precautions the stranger had taken were to veil his retreat to the reaches of the mountain side.

Had he expected any trailer to make a flanking move from up that slope where the Apaches now lay? Travis' teeth nipped the weathered skin of his forearm. Could it be that at some time during the day's journeying the fugitive had doubled back, having seen his trackers? But there had been no traces of any such scouting, and the coyotes would surely have warned them. Human eyes and ears could be tricked, but Travis trusted the senses of Naginlta and Nalik'ideyu far above his own.

No, he did not believe that the rider expected the Apaches. But the man did expect someone or something which would come upon him from the heights. The heights . . . Travis rolled his head slightly to look at the upper reaches of the hills about him—with suspicion.

In their own journey across the mountains and through the pass they had found nothing threatening. Dangerous animals might roam there. There had been some paw marks, one such trail the coyotes had warned against. But the type of precautions the stranger had taken were against intelligent, thinking beings, not against animals more likely to track by scent than by sight.

And if the stranger expected an attack from above, then Travis and Tsoay must be alert. Travis analyzed each feature of the hillside, setting in his mind a picture of every inch of ground they must cross. Just as he had wanted daylight as an ally before, so now was he willing to wait for the shadows of twilight.

He closed his eyes in a final check, able to recall the details of the hiding place, knowing that he could reach it when the conditions favored, without mistake. Then he edged back from his vantage point, and raising his fingers to his lips, made a small angry chittering, three times repeated. One of the species inhabiting these heights, as they had noted earlier, was a creature about as big as the palm of a man's hand, resembling nothing as much as a round ball of ruffled feathers, though its covering might actually have been a silky, fluffy fur. Its short legs could cover ground at an amazing speed, and it had the bold impudence of a creature with few natural enemies. This was its usual cry.

Tsoay's hand waved Travis on to where the younger man had taken position behind the bleached trunk of a fallen tree.

"He hides," Tsoay whispered.

"Against trouble from above." Travis added his own observation.

"But not us, I think."

So Tsoay had come to that conclusion too? Travis tried to gauge the nearness of twilight. There was a period after the passing of Topaz' sun when the dusky light played odd tricks with shadows. That would be the first time for their move. He said as much, and Tsoay nodded eagerly. They sat with their backs to a boulder, the tree trunk serving as a screen, and chewed methodically on ration tablets. There was energy and sustenance in the tasteless squares which would support men, even though their stomachs continued to demand the satisfaction of fresh meat.

Taking turns, they dozed a little. But the last banners of Topaz' sun were still in the sky when Travis judged the shadows cover enough. He had no way of knowing how the stranger was armed. Though he used a horse for transportation, he might well carry a rifle and the most modern Terran sidearms.

The Apaches' bows were little use for infighting, but they had their knives. However, Travis wanted to take the fugitive unharmed if he could. There was information he must have. So he did not even draw his knife as he started downhill.

When he reached a pool of violet dusk at the bottom of the small ravine Naginlta's eyes regarded him knowingly. Travis signaled with his hand and thought out what would be the coyotes' part in this surprise attack. The prick-eared silhouette vanished. Uphill the chitter of a fluff-fur sounded twice— Tsoay was in position.

A howl . . . wailing . . . sobbing . . . was heard, one of the keening songs of the *mba'a*. Travis darted forward. He heard the nicker of a frightened horse, a clicking which could have marked the pawing of hoof on gravel, saw the brush hiding the stranger's hole tremble, a portion of it fall away.

Travis sped on, his moccasins making no sound on the ground. One of the coyotes gave tongue for the second time, the eerie wailing rising to a yapping which echoed from the rocks about them. Travis poised for a dive.

Another section of those artfully heaped branches had given way and a horse reared, its upflung head plainly marked against the sky. A blurred figure weaved back and forth before it, trying to control the mount. The stranger had his hands full, certainly no weapon drawn—this was it!

Travis leaped. His hands found their mark, the shoulders of the stranger. There was a shrill cry from the other as he tried to turn in the Apache's hold, to face his attacker. But Travis bore them both on, rolling almost under the feet of the horse, sliding downhill, the unknown's writhing body pinned down by the Apache's weight and his clasp, tight as an iron grip, about the other's chest and upper arms.

He felt his opponent go limp, but was suspicious enough not to release that hold, for the heavy breathing of the stranger was not that of an unconscious man. They lay so, the unknown still tight in Travis' hold but no longer fighting. The Apache could hear Tsoay soothing the horse with the purring words of a practiced horseman.

Still the stranger did not resume the struggle. They could not lie in this position all night, Travis thought with a wry twist of amusement. He shifted his hold, and got the lightning-quick response he had expected. But it was not quite quick enough, for Travis had the other's hands behind his back, cupping slender, almost delicate wrists together.

"Throw me a cord!" he called to Tsoay.

The younger man ran up with an extra bow cord, and in a moment they had bonds on the struggling captive. Travis rolled their catch over, reaching down for a fistful of hair to pull the head into a patch of clear light.

In his grasp that hair came loose, a braid unwinding. He grunted as he looked down into the stranger's face. Dust marks were streaked now with tear runnels, but the gray eyes which turned fiercely on him said that their owner cried more in rage than fear.

His captive might be wearing long trousers tucked into curved, toed boots, and a loose overblouse, but she was certainly not only a woman, but a very young and attractive one. Also, at the present moment, an exceedingly angry one. And behind that anger was fear, the fear of one fighting hopelessly against insurmountable odds. But as she eyed Travis now her expression changed.

He felt she had expected another captor altogether and was astounded at the sight of him. Her tongue touched her lips, moistening them, and now the fear in her was another kind—the wary fear of one facing a totally new and perhaps dangerous thing.

"Who are you?" Travis spoke in English, for he had no doubts that she was Terran.

Now she sucked in her breath with a gasp of pure astonishment.

"Who are *you?*" she parroted his question in a marked accent. English was not her native tongue, he was sure.

Travis reached out, and again his hands closed on her shoulders. She started to twist and then realized he was merely pulling her up to a sitting position. Some of the fear had left her eyes, an intent interest taking its place.

"You are not Sons of the Blue Wolf," she stated in her heavily accented speech.

Travis smiled. "I am the Fox, not the Wolf," he returned. "And the Coyote is my brother." He snapped his fingers at the shadows, and the two animals came noiselessly into sight. Her gaze widened even more at Naginlta and Nalik'ideyu, and she deduced the bond which must exist between her captor and the beasts.

"This woman is also of our world." Tsoay spoke in Apache, looking over their prisoner with frank interest. "Only she is not of the People."

Sons of the Blue Wolf? Travis thought again of the embroidery designs on the jacket. Who had called themselves by that picturesque title—where—and when in time?

"What do you fear, Daughter of the Blue Wolf?" he asked.

And with that question he seemed to touch some button activating terror. She flung back her head so that she could see the darkening sky.

"The flyer!" Her voice was muted as if more than a whisper would carry to the stars just coming into brilliance above them. "They will come . . . tracking. I did not reach the inner mountains in time."

There was a despairing note in that which cut through to Travis, who found that he, too, was searching the sky, not knowing what he looked for or what kind of menace it promised, only that it was real danger.

VI

"THE NIGHT COMES," Tsoay spoke slowly in English. "Do these you fear hunt in the dark?"

She shook her head to free her forehead from a coil of braid, pulled loose in her struggle with Travis.

"They do not need eyes or such noses as those four-footed hunters of yours. They have a machine to track—"

"Then what purpose is this brush pile of yours?" Travis raised his chin at the disturbed hiding place.

"They do not constantly use the machine, and one can hope. But at night they can ride on its beam. We are not far enough into the hills to lose them. Bahatur went lame, and so I was slowed. . . ."

"And what lies in these mountains that those you fear dare not invade them?" Travis continued.

"I do not know, save if one can climb far enough inside, one is safe from pursuit."

"I ask it again: Who are you?" The Apache leaned forward, his face in the fast-fading light now only inches away from hers. She did not shrink from his close scrutiny but met him eye to eye. This was a woman of proud independence, truly a chief's daughter, Travis decided.

"I am of the People of the Blue Wolf. We were brought across the star lanes to make this world safe for . . . for . . . the . . ." She hesitated, and now there was a shade of puzzlement on her face. "There is a reason—a dream. No, there is the dream and there is reality. I am Kaydessa of the Golden Horde, but sometimes I remember other things—like this speech of strange words I am mouthing now—"

"The Golden Horde!" Travis knew now. The embroidery, Sons of the Blue Wolf, all fitted into a special pattern. But what a pattern! Scythian art, the ornament that the warriors of Genghis Khan bore so proudly. Tatars, Mongols—the barbarians who had swept from the fastness of the steppes to change the course of history, not only in Asia but across the plains of middle Europe. The men of the Emperor Khans who had ridden behind the vak-tailed standards of Genghis Khan, Kublai, Tamerlane—!

"The Golden Horde," Travis repeated once again. "That lies far back in the history of another world, Wolf Daughter."

She stared at him, a queer, lost expression of her dust-grimed face.

"I know." Her voice was so muted he could hardly distinguish the words. "My people live in two times, and many do not realize that."

Tsoay had crouched down beside them to listen. Now he put out his hand, touching Travis's shoulder.

"Redax?"

"Or its like." For Travis was sure of one point. The project, which had been training three teams for space colonization—one of Eskimos, one of Pacific Islanders, and one of his own Apaches—had no reason or chance to select Mongols from the wild past of the raiding Hordes. There was only one nation on Terra which could have picked such colonists.

"You are Russian." He studied her carefully, intent on noting the effect of his words.

But she did not lose that lost look. "Russian . . . Russian . . ." she repeated, as if the very word was strange.

Travis was alarmed. Any Russian colony planted here could well possess technicians with machines capable of tracking a fugitive, and if mountain heights were protection against such a hunt, he intended to gain them, even by night traveling. He said this to Tsoay, and the other emphatically agreed.

"The horse is too lame to go on," the younger man reported.

Travis hesitated for a long second. Since the time they had stolen their first mounts from the encroaching Spanish, horses had always been wealth to his people. To leave an animal which could well serve the clan was not right. But they dared not waste time with a lame beast.

"Leave it here, free," he ordered.

"And the woman?"

"She goes with us. We must learn all we can of these people and what they do here. Listen, Wolf Daughter," again Travis leaned close to make sure she was listening to him as he spoke with emphasis—"you will travel with us into these high places, and there will be no trouble from you." He drew his knife and held the blade warningly before her eyes.

"It was already in my mind to go to the mountains,'' she told him evenly. ''Untie my hands, brave warrior, you have surely nothing to fear from a woman.''

His hand made a swift sweep and plucked a knife as long and keen as his from the folds of the sash beneath her loose outer garment.

''Not now, Wolf Daughter, since I have drawn your fangs.''

He helped her to her feet and slashed the cord about her wrists with her knife, which he then fastened to his own belt. Alerting the coyotes, he dispatched them ahead; and the three started on, the Mongol girl between the two Apaches. The abandoned horse nickered lonesomely and then began to graze on tufts of grass, moving slowly to favor his foot.

The two moons rode the sky as the hours advanced, their beams fighting the shadows. Travis felt reasonably safe from any attack at ground level, depending upon the coyotes for warning. But he held them all to a steady pace. And he did not question the girl again until all three of them hunkered down at a small mountain spring, to dash icy water over their faces and drink, from cupped hands.

''Why do you flee your own people, Wolf Daughter?''

''My name is Kaydessa,'' she corrected him.

He chuckled with laughter at the prim tone of her voice. ''And you see here Tsoay of the People—the Apaches—while I am Fox.'' He was giving her the English equivalent of his tribal name.

''Apaches.'' She tried to repeat the word with the same accent he had used. ''And what are Apaches?''

''Indians—Amerindians,'' he explained. ''But

you have not answered my question, Kaydessa. Why do you run from your own people?''

"Not from my people,'' she said, shaking her head determinedly. "From those others. It is like this—Oh, how can I make you understand rightly?'' She spread her wet hands out before her in the moonlight, the damp patches on her sleeves clinging to her arms. "There are my people of the Golden Horde, though once we were different and we can remember bits of that previous life. Then there are also the men who live in the sky ship and use the machine so that we think only the thoughts they would have us think. Now why,'' she looked at Travis intently—"do I wish to tell you all this? It is strange. You say you are Indian—American—are we then enemies? There is a part memory which says that we are . . . were . . .''

"Let us rather say,'' he corrected her, "that the Apaches and the Horde are not enemies here and now, no matter what was before.'' That was the truth, Travis recognized. By all accounts his people had come out of Asia in the very dim beginnings of migrating peoples. For all her dark-red hair and gray eyes, this girl who had been arbitrarily returned to a past just as they had been by Redax, could well be a distant clancousin.

"You—'' Kaydessa's fingers rested for a moment on his wrist—"you, too, were sent here from across the stars. Is this not so?''

"It is so.''

"And there are those here who govern you now?''

"No. We are free.''

"How did you become free?'' she demanded fiercely.

67

Travis hesitated. He did not want to tell of the wrecked ship, the fact that his people possessed no real defenses against the Russian-controlled colony.

"We went to the mountains," he replied evasively.

"Your governing machine failed?" Kaydessa laughed. "Ah, they are so great, those men of the machines. But they are smaller and weaker when their machines cannot obey them."

"It is so with your camp?" Travis probed gently. He was not quite sure of her meaning, but he dared not ask more detailed questions without dangerously revealing his own ignorance.

"In some manner their control machine—it can only work upon those within a certain distance. They discovered that in the days of the first landing, when hunters went out freely and many of them did not return. After that when hunters were sent out to learn how lay this land, they went along in the flyer with a machine so that there would be no more escapes. But we knew!" Kaydessa's fingers curled into small fists. "Yes, we knew that if we could get beyond the machines, there was freedom for us. And we planned—many of us—planned. Then nine or ten sleeps ago those others were very excited. They gathered in their ship, watching their machines. And something happened. For a while all those machines went dead.

"Jagatai, Kuchar, my brother Hulagur, Menlik . . ." She was counting the names off on her fingers. "They raided the horse herd, rode out . . ."

"And you?"

"I, too, should have ridden. But there was Aljar,

my sister—Kuchar's wife. She was very near her time and to ride thus, fleeing and fast, might kill her and the child. So I did not go. Her son was born that night, but the others had the machine at work once more. We might long to go here," she brought her fist up to her breast, and then raised it to her head—"but there was that *here* which kept us to the camp and their will. We only knew that if we could reach the mountains, we might find our people who had already gained their freedom."

"But you are here. How did you escape?" Tsoay wanted to know.

"They knew that I would have gone had it not been for Aljar. So they said they would make her ride out with them unless I played guide to lead them to my brother and the others. Then I knew I must take up the sword of duty and hunt with them. But I prayed that the spirits of the upper air look with favor upon me, and they granted aid. . . ." Her eyes held a look of wonder. "For when we were out on the plains and well away from the settlement, a grass devil attacked the leader of the searching party, and he dropped the mind control and so it was broken. Then I rode. Blue Sky Above knows how I rode. And those others are not with their horses as are the people of the Wolf."

"When did this happen?"

"Three suns ago."

Travis counted back in his mind. Her date for the failure of the machine in the Russian camp seemed to coincide with the crash landing of the American ship. Had one thing any connection with the other? It was very possible. The planeting spacer might have fought some kind of weird duel with the other colony before it plunged to earth on the other side of the mountain range.

"Do you know where in these mountains your people hide?"

Kaydessa shook her head. "Only that I must head south, and when I reach the highest peak make a signal fire on the north slope. But that I cannot do now, for those in the flyer may see it. I know they are on my trail, for twice I have seen it. Listen, Fox, I ask this of you—I, Kaydessa, who am eldest daughter to the Khan—for you are like unto us, a warrior and a brave man, that I believe. It may be that you cannot be governed by their machine, for you have not rested under their spell, nor are of our blood. Therefore, if they come close enough to send forth the call, the call I must obey as if I were a slave dragged upon a horse rope, then do you bind my hands and feet and hold me here, no matter how much I struggle to follow that command. For that which is truly me does not want to go. Will you swear this by the fires which expel demons?"

The utter sincerity of her tone convinced Travis that she was pleading for aid against a danger she firmly believed in. Whether she was right about his immunity to the Russian mental control was another matter, and one he would rather not put to the test.

"We do not swear by the fires, Blue Wolf Maiden, but by the Path of the Lightning." His fingers moved as if to curl about the sacred charred wood his people had once carried as "medicine." "So do I promise!"

She looked at him for a long moment and then nodded in satisfaction.

They left the pool and pushed on toward the mountain slopes, working their way back to the pass. A low growl out of the dark brought them to an instant halt. Naginlta's warning was sharp; there was danger ahead, acute danger.

The moonlight from the moons made a weird pattern of light and dark on the stretch ahead. Anything from a slinking four-footed hunter to a war party of intelligent beings might have been lying in wait there.

A flitting shadow out of shadows. Nalik'ideyu pressed against Travis' legs, making a barrier of her warm body, attracting his attention to a spot at the left perhaps a hundred yards on. There was a great splotch of dark there, large enough to hide a really formidable opponent; that wordless communication between animal and man told Travis that such an opponent was just what was lurking there.

Whatever lay in ambush beside the upper track was growing impatient as its destined prey ceased to advance, the coyotes reported.

"Your left—beyond that pointed rock—in the big shadow—"

"Do you see it?" Tsoay demanded.

"No. But the *mba'a* do."

The men had their bows ready, arrows set to the cords. But in this light such weapons were practically useless unless the enemy moved into the path of the moon.

"What is it?" Kaydessa asked in a half whisper.

"Something waits for us ahead."

Before he could stop her, she set her fingers to her lips and gave a piercing whistle.

There was answering movement in the shadow.

Travis shot at that, his arrow followed instantly by one from Tsoay. There was a cry, scaling up in a throat-scalding scream which made Travis flinch. Not because of the sound, but because of the hint which lay behind it—could it have been a human cry?

The thing flopped out into a patch of moonlight. It was four-limbed, its body silvery—and it was large. But the worst was that it had been groveling on all fours when it fell, and now it was rising on its hind feet, one forepaw striking madly at the two arrows dancing head-deep in its upper shoulder. Man? No! But something sufficiently manlike to chill the three downtrail.

A whirling four-footed hunter dashed in, snapped at the creature's legs, and it squalled again, aiming a blow with a forepaw; but the attacking coyote was already gone. Together Naginlta and Nalik'ideyu were harassing the creature, just as they had fought the split horn, giving the hunters time to shoot. Travis, although he again felt that touch of horror and disgust he could not account for, shot again.

Between them the Apaches must have sent a dozen arrows into the raving beast before it went to its knees and Naginlta sprang for its throat. Even then the coyote yelped and flinched, a bleeding gash across its head from the raking talons of the dying thing. When it no longer moved, Travis approached to see more closely what they had brought down. That smell . . .

Just as the embroidery on Kaydessa's jacket had awakened memories from his Terran past, so did this stench remind him of something. Where—when— had he smelled it before? Travis connected it with dark, dark and danger. Then he gasped in a half exclamation.

Not on this world, no, but on two others: two worlds of that broken stellar empire where he had been an involuntary explorer two planet years ago! The beast things which had lived in the dark of the desert world the Terrans' wandering galactic derelict had landed upon. Yes, the beast things whose nature they had never been able to deduce. Were they the degenerate dregs of a once intelligent species? Or were they animals, akin to man, but still animals?

The ape-things had controlled the night of the desert world. And they had been met again—also in the dark—in the ruins of the city which had been the final goal of the ship's taped voyage. So they were a part of the vanished civilization. And Travis' own vague surmise concerning Topaz was proven correct. This had not been an empty world for the long-gone space people. This planet had a purpose and a use, or else this beast would not have been here.

"Devil!" Kaydessa made a face of disgust.

"You know it?" Tsoay asked Travis. "What is it?"

"That I do not know, but it is a thing left over from the star people's time. And I have seen it on two other of their worlds."

"A man?" Tsoay surveyed the body critically. "It wears no clothes, has no weapons, but it walks erect. It looks like an ape, a very big ape. It is not a good thing, I think."

"If it runs with a pack—as they do elsewhere—this could be a very bad thing." Travis, remembering how these creatures had attacked in force on the other worlds, looked about him apprehensively. Even with the coyotes on guard, they could not stand up to such a pack closing in through the dark. They had better hole up in some defendable place and wait out the rest of the night.

Naginlta brought them to a cliff overhang where they could set their backs to the hard rock of the mountain, face outward to a space they could cover with arrow flight if the need arose. And the coyotes, lying before them with their noses resting on paws, would, Travis knew, alert them long before the enemy could close in.

They huddled against the rock, Kaydessa between them, alert at first to every sound of the night, their hearts beating faster at a small scrape of gravel, the rustle of a bush. Slowly, they began to relax.

"It is well that two sleep while one guards," Travis observed. "By morning we must push on, out of this country."

So the Apaches shared the watch in turn, the Tatar girl at first protesting, and then falling exhausted into a slumber which left her breathing heavily.

Travis, on the dawn watch, began to speculate about the ape-thing they had killed. The two previous times he had met this creature it had been in ruins of the old empire. Were there ruins somewhere here? He wanted to make sure about that. On the other hand, there was the problem of the Tatar-Mongol settlement controlled by the Reds. There was no doubt in his mind that, were the Reds to suspect the existence of the Apache camp, they would make every attempt to hunt down and kill or capture the survivors from the American ship. A warning must be carried to the rancheria as quickly as they could make the return trip.

Beside him the girl stirred, raising her head. Travis glanced at her and then watched with attention. She was looking straight ahead, her eyes as fixed as if she were in a trance. Now she inched forward from the mountain wall, wriggling out of its shelter.

"What—?" Tsoay had awakened again. But Travis was already moving. He pushed on, rushing up to stand beside her, shoulder to shoulder.

"What is it? Where do you go?" he asked.

She made no answer, did not even seem aware of his voice. He caught at her arm and she pulled to free herself. When he tightened his grip she did not fight him actively as during their first encounter, but merely pulled and twisted as if she were being compelled to go ahead.

Compulsion! He remembered her plea the night before, asking his help against recapture by the machine. Now he deliberately tripped her, twisted her hands behind her back. She swayed in his hold, trying to win to her feet, paying no attention to him save as a hindrance against her answering that demanding call he could not hear.

VII

"WHAT HAPPENED?" Tsoay took a swift stride, stood over the writhing girl whose strength was now such that Travis had to exert all his efforts to control her.

"I think that the machine she spoke about is holding her. She is being drawn to it out of hiding as one draws a calf on a rope."

Both coyotes had arisen and were watching the struggle with interest, but there was no warning from them. Whatever called Kaydessa into such mindless and will-less answer did not touch the animals. And neither Apache felt it. So perhaps only Kaydessa's people were subject to it, as she had thought. How far away was that machine? Not too near, for otherwise the coyotes would have traced the man or men operating it.

"We cannot move her," Tsoay brought the problem into the open—"unless we bind and carry her. She is one of their kind. Why not let her go to them, unless you fear she will talk." His hand went to the knife in his belt, and Travis knew what primitive impulse moved in the younger man.

In the old days a captive who was likely to give

trouble was efficiently eliminated. In Tsoay that memory was awake now. Travis shook his head.

"She has said that others of her kin are in these hills. We must not set two wolf packs hunting us," Travis said, giving the more practical reason which might better appeal to the savage instinct for self-preservation. "But you are right, since she has tried to answer this summons, we cannot force her with us. Therefore, do you take the back trail. Tell Buck what we have discovered and have him make the necessary precautions against either these Mongol outlaws or a Red thrust over the mountains."

"And you?"

"I stay to discover where the outlaws hide and learn all I can of this settlement. We may have reason to need friends—"

"Friends!" Tsoay spat. "The People need no friends! If we have warning, we can hold our own country! As the Pinda-lick-o-yi have discovered before."

"Bows and arrows against guns and machines?" Travis inquired bitingly. "We must know more before we make any warrior boasts for the future. Tell Buck what we have discovered. Also say I will join you before," Travis calculated—"ten suns. If I do not, send no search party; the clan is too small to risk more lives for one."

"And if these Reds take you—?"

Travis grinned, not pleasantly. "They shall learn nothing! Can their machines sort out the thoughts of a dead man?" He did not intend his future to end as abruptly as that, but also he would not be easy meat for any Red hunting party.

Tsoay took a share of their rations and refused the

company of the coyotes. Travis realized that for all his seeming ease with the animals, the younger scout had little more liking for them than Deklay and the others back at the rancheria. Tsoay went at dawn, aiming at the pass.

Travis sat down beside Kaydessa. They had bound her to a small tree, and she strove incessantly to free herself, turning her head at an acute and painful angle, only to face the same direction in which she had been tied. There was no breaking the spell which held her. And she would soon wear herself out with that struggling. Then he struck an expert blow.

The girl sagged limply, and he untied her. It all depended now on the range of the beam or broadcast of that diabolical machine. From the attitude of the coyotes, he assumed that those using the machine had not made any attempt to come close. They might not even know where their quarry was; they would simply sit and wait in the foothills for the caller to reel in a helpless captive.

Travis thought that if he moved Kaydessa farther away from that point, sooner or later they would be out of range and she would awake from the knock-out, free again. Although she was not light, he could manage to carry her for a while. So burdened, Travis started on, with the coyotes scouting ahead.

He speedily discovered that he had set himself an ambitious task. The going was rough, and carrying the girl reduced his advance to a snail-paced crawl. But it gave him time to make careful plans.

As long as the Reds held the balance of power on this side of the mountain range, the rancheria was in danger. Bows and knives against modern armament was no contest at all. And it would only be a matter of time before exploration on the part of the northern settlement—or some tracking down of Tatar fugitives—would bring the enemy across the pass.

The Apaches could move farther south into the unknown continent below the wrecked ship, thus prolonging the time before they were discovered. But that would only postpone the inevitable showdown. Whether Travis could make his clan believe that, was also a matter of concern.

On the other hand, if the Red overlords could be met in some practical way . . . Travis' mind fastened on that more attractive idea, worrying it as Naginlta worried a prey, tearing out and devouring the more delicate portions. Every bit of sense and prudence argued against such an approach, whose success could rest only between improbability and impossibility; yet that was the direction in which he longed to move.

Across his shoulder Kaydessa stirred and moaned. The Apache doubled his efforts to reach the outcrop of rock he could see ahead, chiseled into high relief by the winds. In its lee they would have protection from any sighting from below. Panting, he made it, lowering the girl into the guarded cup of space, and waited.

She moaned again, lifted one hand to her head. Her eyes were half open, and still he could not be sure whether they focused on him and her surroundings intelligently or not.

"Kaydessa!"

Her heavy eyelids lifted, and he had no doubt she could see him. But there was no recognition of his identity in her gaze, only surprise and fear—the same expression she had worn during their first meeting in the foothills.

"Daughter of the Wolf," he spoke slowly. "Remember!" Travis made that an order, an emphatic appeal to the mind under the influence of the caller.

She frowned, the struggle she was making naked on her face. Then she answered:

"You—Fox—"

Travis grunted with relief, his alarm subsiding. Then she *could* remember.

"Yes," he responded eagerly.

But she was gazing about, her puzzlement growing. "Where is this—?"

"We are higher in the mountains."

Now fear was pushing out bewilderment. "How did I come here?"

"I brought you." Swiftly he outlined what had happened at their night camp.

The hand which had been at her head was now pressed tight across her lips as if she were biting furiously into its flesh to still some panic of her own, and her gray eyes were round and haunted.

"You are free now," Travis said.

Kaydessa nodded, and then dropped her hand to speak. "You brought me away from the hunters. You did not have to obey them?"

"I heard nothing."

"You do not hear—you feel!" She shuddered. "Please." She clawed at the stone beside her, pulling up to her feet. "Let us go—let us go quickly! They will try again—move farther in—"

"Listen," Travis had to be sure of one thing— "have they any way of knowing that they had you under control and that you have again escaped?"

Kaydessa shook her head, some of the panic again shadowing her eyes.

"Then we'll just go on—" his chin lifted to the wastelands before them—"try to keep out of their reach."

And away from the pass to the south, he told himself silently. He dared not lead the enemy to that secret, so he must travel west or hole up somewhere in this unknown wilderness until they could be sure Kaydessa was no longer susceptible to that call, or that they were safely beyond its beamed radius. There was the chance of contacting her outlaw kin, just as there was the chance of stumbling into a pack of the ape-things. Before dark they must discover a protected camp site.

They needed water, food. He had a bare half dozen ration tablets. But the coyotes could locate water.

"Come!" Travis beckoned to Kaydessa, motioning her to climb ahead of him so that he could watch for any indication of her succumbing once again to the influence of the enemy. But his burdened early morning flight had told on Travis more than he thought, and he discovered he could not spur himself on to a pace better than a walk. Now and again one of the coyotes, usually Nalik'ideyu, would come into view, express impatience in both stance and mental signal, and then be gone again. The Apache was increasingly aware that the animals were disturbed, yet to his tentative gropings at contact they did not reply. Since they gave no warning of hostile animal or man, he could only be on constant guard, watching the countryside about him.

They had been following a ledge for several minutes before Travis was aware of some strange features of that path. Perhaps he had actually noted them with a trained eye before his archaeological studies of the recent past gave him a reason for the faint marks. This crack in the mountain's skin might have begun as a natural fault, but afterward it had been worked with tools, smoothed, widened to serve the purpose of some form of intelligence!

Travis caught at Kaydessa's shoulder to slow her pace. He could not have told why he did not want to speak aloud here, but he felt the need for silence. She glanced around, perplexed, more so when he went down on his knees and ran his fingers along one of those ancient tool marks. He was certain it was very old. Inside of him anticipation bubbled. A road made with such labor could only lead to something of importance. He was going to make the discovery, the dream which had first drawn him into these mountains.

"What is it?" Kaydessa knelt beside him, frowning at the ledge.

"This was cut by someone, a long time ago," Travis half whispered and then wondered why. There was no reason to believe the road makers could hear him when perhaps a thousand years or more lay between the chipping of that stone and this day.

The Tatar girl looked over her shoulder. Perhaps she too was troubled by the sense that here time was subtly telescoped, that past and present might be meeting. Or was that feeling with them both because of their enforced conditioning?

"Who?" Now her voice sank in turn.

"Listen—" he regarded her intently—"did your

people or the Reds ever find any traces of the old civilization here—ruins?"

"No." She leaned forward, tracing with her own finger the same almost-obliterated marks which had intrigued Travis. "But I think they have looked. Before they discovered that we could be free, they sent out parties—to hunt, they said—but afterward they always asked many questions about the country. Only they never asked about ruins. Is that what they wished us to find? But why? Of what value are old stones piled on one another?"

"In themselves, little save for the knowledge they may give us of the people who piled them. But for what the stones might contain—much value!"

"And how do you know what they might contain, Fox?"

"Because I have seen such treasure houses of the star men," he returned absently. To him the marks on the ledge were a pledge of greater discoveries to come. He must find where that carefully constructed road ran—to what it led. "Let us see where this will take us."

But first he gave the chittering signal in four sharp bursts. And the tawny-gray bodies came out of the tangled brush, bounding up to the ledge. Together the coyotes faced him, their attention all for his halting communication.

Ruins might lie ahead; he hoped that they did. But on another planet such ruins had twice proved to be deadly traps, and only good fortune had prevented their closing on Terran explorers. If the ape-things or any other dangerous form of life had taken up residence before them, he wanted good warning.

Together the coyotes turned and loped along the

now level way of the ledge, disappearing around a curve fitted to the mountain side while Travis and Kaydessa followed.

They heard it before they saw its source—a water-fall. Probably not a large one, but high. Rounding the curve, they came into a fine mist of spray where sunlight made rainbows of color across a filmy veil of water.

For a long moment they stood entranced. Kaydessa then gave a little cry, held out her hands to the purling mist and brought them to her lips again to suck the gathered moisture.

Water slicked the surface of the ledge, and Travis pushed her back against the wall of the cliff. As far as he could discern, their road continued behind the outflung curtain of water, and footing on the wet stone was treacherous. With their backs to the solid security of the wall, facing outward into the solid drape of water, they edged behind it and came out into rainbowed sunlight again.

Here either provident nature or ancient art had hollowed a pocket in the stone which was filled with water. They drank. Then Travis filled his canteen while Kaydessa washed her face, holding the cold freshness of the moisture to her cheeks with both palms.

She spoke, but he could not hear her through the roar. She leaned closer and raised her voice to a half shout.

"This is a place of spirits! Do you not also feel their power, Fox?"

Perhaps for a space out of time he did feel some-thing. This was a watering place, perhaps a never-ceasing watering place—and to his desert-born-

and-bred race all water was a spirit gift never to be taken for granted. The rainbow—the Spirit People's sacred sign—old beliefs stirred in Travis, moving him. "I feel," he said, nodding in emphasis to his agreement.

They followed the ledge road to a section where a landslide of an earlier season had choked it. Travis worked a careful way across the debris, Kaydessa obeying his guidance in turn. Then they were on a sloping downward way which led to a staircase—the treads weather-worn and crumbling, the angle so steep Travis wondered if it had ever been intended for beings with a physique approximating the Terrans'

They came to a cleft where an arch of stone was chiseled out as a roofing. Travis thought he could make out a trace of carving on the capstone, so worn by years and weather that it was now only a faint shadow of design.

The cleft was a door into another valley. Here, too, golden mist swirled in tendrils to disguise and cloak what stood there. Travis had found his ruins. Only the structures were intact, not breached by time.

Mist flowed in lapping tongues back and forth, confusing outlines, now shuttering, now baring oval windows which were spaced in diamonds of four on round tower surfaces. There were no visible cracks, no cloaking of climbing vegetation, nothing to suggest age and long roots in the valley. Nor did the architecture he could view match any he had seen on those other worlds.

Travis strode away from the cleft doorway. Under his moccasins was a block pavement, yellow and green stone set in a simple pattern of checks. This, too, was level, unchipped and undisturbed save for a drift or two of soil driven in by the wind. And nowhere could he see any vegetation.

The towers were of the same green stone as half the pavement blocks, a glassy green which made him think of jade—if jade could be mined in such quantities as these five-story towers demanded.

Nalik'ideyu padded to him, and he could hear the faint click of her claws on the pavement. There was a deep silence in this place, as if the air itself swallowed and digested all sound. The wind which had been with them all the day of their journeying was left beyond the cleft.

Yet there was life here. The coyote told him that in her own way. She had not made up her mind concerning that life—wariness and curiosity warred in her now as her pointed muzzle lifted toward the windows overhead.

The windows were all well above ground level, but there was no opening in the first stories as far as Travis could see. He debated moving into the range of those windows to investigate the far side of the towers for doorways. The mist and the message from Nalik'ideyu nourished his suspicions. Out in the open he would be too good a target for whatever or whoever might be standing within the deep-welled frames.

The silence was shattered by a boom. Travis jumped, slewed half around, knife in hand.

Boom-boom . . . a second heavy beat-beat . . . then a clangor with a swelling echo.

Kaydessa flung back her head and called, her voice rising up as if funneled by the valley walls. She then whistled as she had done when they fronted the ape-thing and ran on to catch at Travis' sleeve, her face eager.

"My people! Come—it is my people!"

She tugged him on before breaking into a run, weaving fearlessly around the base of one of the towers. Travis ran after her, afraid he might lose her in the mist.

Three towers, another stretch of open pavement, and then the mist lifted to show them a second carved doorway not two hundred yards ahead. The boom-boom seemed to pull Kaydessa and Travis could do nothing but trail her, the coyotes now trotting beside him.

VIII

THEY BURST through a last wide band of mist into a wilderness of tall grass and shrubs. Travis heard the coyotes give tongue, but it was too late. Out of nowhere whirled a leather loop, settling about his chest, snapping his arms tight to his body, taking him off his feet with a jerk to be dragged helplessly along the ground behind a galloping horse.

A tawny fury sprang in the air to snap at the horse's head. Travis kicked fruitlessly, trying to regain his feet as the horse reared, and fought against the control of his shouting rider. All through the melee the Apache heard Kaydessa shrilly screaming words he did not understand.

Travis was on his knees, coughing in the dust, exerting the muscles in his chest and shoulders to loosen the lariat. On either side of him the coyotes wove a snarling pattern of defiance, dashing back and forth to present no target for the enemy, yet keeping the excited horses so stirred up that their riders could use neither ropes nor blades.

Then Kaydessa ran between two of the ringing horses to Travis and jerked at the loop about him.

The tough, braided leather eased its hold, and he was able to gasp in full lungfuls of air. She was still shouting, but the tone had changed from one of recognition to a defnite scolding.

Travis won to his feet just as the rider who had lassoed him finally got his horse under rein and dismounted. Holding the rope, the man walked hand over hand toward them, as Travis back on the Arizona range would have approached a nervous, unschooled pony.

The Mongol was an inch or so shorter than the Apache, and his face was young, though he had a drooping mustache bracketing his mouth with slender spear points of black hair. His breeches were tucked into high red boots, and he wore a loose felt jacket patterned with the same elaborate embroidery Travis had seen on Kaydessa's. On his head was a hat with a wide fur border—in spite of the heat—and that too bore touches of scarlet and gold design.

Still holding his lariat, the Mongol reached Kaydessa and stood for a moment, eyeing her up and down before he asked a question. She gave an impatient twitch to the rope. The coyotes snarled, but the Apache thought the animals no longer considered the danger immediate.

"This is my brother Hulagur." Kaydessa made the introduction over her shoulder. "He does not have your speech."

Hulagur not only did not understand, he was also impatient. He jerked at the rope with such sudden force that Travis was almost thrown. Then Kaydessa dragged as fiercely on the lariat in the other direction and burst into a soaring harangue which drew the rest of the men closer.

Travis flexed his upper arms, and the slack gained by Kaydessa's action made the lariat give again. He studied the Tatar outlaws. There were five of them beside Hulagur, lean men, hard-faced, narrow-eyed, the ragged clothing of three pieced out with scraps of hide. Besides the swords with the curved blades, they were armed with bows, two to each man, one long, one shorter. One of the riders carried a lance, long tassels of woolly hair streaming from below its head. Travis saw in them a formidable array of barbaric fighting men, but he thought that man for man the Apaches could not only take on the Mongols with confidence, but might well defeat them.

The Apache had never been a hot-headed, ride-for-glory fighter like the Cheyenne, the Sioux, and the Comanche of the open plains. He estimated the odds against him, used ambush, trick, and every feature of the countryside as weapon and defense. Fifteen Apache fighting men under Chief Geronimo had kept five thousand American and Mexican troops in the field for a year and had come off victorious for the moment.

Travis knew the tales of Genghis Khan and his formidable generals who swept over Asia into Europe, unbeaten and seemingly undefeatable. But they had been a wild wave, fed by a reservoir of manpower from the steppes of their homeland, utilizing driven walls of captives to protect their own men in city assaults and attacks. He doubted if even that endless sea of men could have won the Arizona desert defended by Apaches under Cochise, Victorio, or Magnus Colorado. The white man had done it—by superior arms and attrition; but bow against bow, knife against sword, craft and cunning against craft and cunning—he did not think so. . . .

Hulagur dropped the end of the lariat, and Kaydessa swung around, loosening the loop so that the rope fell to Travis' feet. The Apache stepped free of it, turned and passed between two of the horsemen to gather up the bow he had dropped. The coyotes had gone with him and when he turned again to face the company of Tartars, both animals crowded past him to the entrance of the valley, plainly urging him to retire there.

The horseman had faced about also, and the warrior with the lance balanced the shaft of the weapon in his hand as if considering the possibility of trying to spear Travis. But just then Kaydessa came up, towing Hulagur by a firm hold on his sash-belt.

"I have told this one," she reported to Travis, "how it is between us and that you also are enemy to those who hunt us. It is well that you sit together beside a fire and talk of these things."

Again that boom-boom broke her speech, coming from farther out in the open land.

"You will do this?" She made of it a half question, half statement.

Travis glanced about him. He could dodge back into the misty valley of the towers before the Tatars could ride him down. However, if he could patch up some kind of truce between his people and the outlaws, the Apaches would have only the Reds from the settlement to watch. Too many times in Terran past had war on two fronts been disastrous.

"I come—carrying this—and not pulled by your ropes." He held up his bow in an exaggerated gesture so that Hulagur could understand.

Coiling the lariat, the Mongol looked from the

Apache bow to Travis. Slowly, and with obvious reluctance, he nodded agreement.

At Hulagur's call the lancer rode up to the waiting Apache, stretched out a booted foot in the heavy stirrup, and held down a hand to bring Travis up behind him riding double. Kaydessa mounted in the same fashion behind her brother.

Travis looked at the coyotes. Together the animals stood in the door to the tower valley, and neither made any move to follow as the horses trotted off. He beckoned with his hand and called to them.

Heads up, they continued to watch him go in company with the Mongols. Then without any reply to his coaxing, they melted back into the mists. For a moment Travis was tempted to slide down and run the risk of taking a lance point between the shoulders as he followed Naginlta and Nalik'ideyu into retreat. He was startled, jarred by the new awareness of how much he had come to depend on the animals. Ordinarily, Travis Fox was not one to be governed by the wishes of a *mba'a*, intelligent and un-animal-like as it might be. This was an affair of men, and coyotes had no part in it!

Half an hour later Travis sat in the outlaw camp. There were fifteen Mongols in sight, a half dozen women and two children adding to the count. On a hillock near their yurts, the round brush-and-hide shelters—not too different from the wickiups of Travis' own people—was a crude drum, a hide stretched taut over a hollowed section of log. And next to that stood a man wearing a tall pointed cap, a red robe, and a girdle from which swung a fringe of small bones, tiny animal skulls, and polished bits of stone and carved wood.

It was this man's efforts which sent the boom-boom sounding at intervals over the landscape. Was this a signal—part of a ritual? Travis was not certain, though he guessed that the drummer was either medicine man or shaman, and so of some power in this company. Such men were credited with the ability to prophesy and also endowed with medium-ship between man and spirit in the old days of the great Hordes.

The Apache evaluated the rest of the company. As was true of his own party, these men were much the same age—young and vigorous. And it was also apparent that Hulagur held a position of some importance among them—if he were not their chief.

After a last resounding roll on the drum, the shaman thrust the sticks into his girdle and came down to the fire at the center of the camp. He was taller than his fellows, pole thin under his robes, his face narrow, clean-shaven, with brows arched by nature to give him an unchanging expression of skepticism. He strode along, his tinkling collection of charms providing him with a not unmusical accompaniment, and came to stand directly before Travis, eyeing him carefully.

Travis copied his silence in what was close to a duel of wills. There was that in the shaman's narrowed green eyes which suggested that if Hulagur did in fact lead these fighting men, he had an advisor of determination and intelligence behind him.

"This is Menlik." Kaydessa did not push past the men to the fireside, but her voice carried.

Hulagur growled at his sister, but his admonition made no impression on her, and she replied in as hot a tone. The shaman's hand went up, silencing both of them.

"You are—who?" Like Kaydessa, Menlik spoke a heavily accented English.

"I am Travis Fox, of the Apaches."

"The Apaches," the shaman repeated. "You are of the West, the American West, then."

"You know much, man of spirit talk."

"One remembers. At times one remembers," Menlik answered almost absently. "How does an Apache find his way across the stars?"

"The same way Menlik and his people did," Travis returned. "You were sent to settle this planet, and so were we."

"There are many more of you?" countered Menlik swiftly.

"Are there not many of the Horde? Would one man, or three, or four, be sent to hold a world?" Travis fenced. "You hold the north, we the south of this land."

"But *they* are not governed by a machine!" Kaydessa cut in. "They are free!"

Menlik frowned at the girl. "Woman, this is a matter for warriors. Keep your tongue silent between your jaws!"

She stamped one foot, standing with her fists on her hips.

"I am a Daughter of the Blue Wolf. And we are all warriors—men and women alike—so shall we be as long as the Horde is not free to ride where we wish! These men have won their freedom; it is well that we learn how."

Menlik's expression did not change, but his lids drooped over his eyes as a murmur of what might be agreement came from the group. More than one of them must have understood enough English to translate for the others. Travis wondered about that. Had these men and women who had outwardly reverted to the life of their nomad ancestors once been well educated in the modern sense, educated enough to learn the basic language of the nation their rulers had set up as their principal enemy?

"So you ride the land south of the mountains?" the shaman continued.

"That is true."

"Then why did you come hither?"

Travis shrugged. "Why does anyone ride or travel into new lands? There is a desire to see what may lie beyond—"

"Or to scout before the march of warriors!" Menlik snapped. "There is no peace between your rulers and mine. Do you ride now to take the herds and pastures of the Horde—or to try to do so?"

Travis turned his head deliberately from side to side, allowing them all to witness his slow and openly contemptuous appraisal of their camp.

"*This* is your Horde, Shaman? Fifteen warriors? Much has changed since the days of Temujin, has it not?"

"What do you know of Temujin—you, who are a man of no ancestors, out of the West?"

"What do I know of Temujin? That he was a leader of warriors and became Genghis Khan, the great lord of the East. But the Apaches had their warlords also, rider of barren lands. And I am of those who raided over two nations when Victorio and Cochise scattered their enemies as a man scatters a handful of dust in the wind."

"You talk bold, Apache. . . ." There was a hint of threat in that.

"I speak as any warrior, Shaman. Or are you so used to talking with spirits instead of men that you do not realize that?"

He might have been alienating the shaman by such a sharp reply, but Travis thought he judged the temper of these people. To face them boldly was the only way to impress them. They would not treat with an inferior, and he was already at a disadvantage coming on foot, without any backing in force, into a territory held by horsemen who were suspicious and jealous of their recently acquired freedom. His only chance was to establish himself as an equal and then try to convince them that Apache and Tatar-Mongol had a common cause against the Reds who controlled the settlement of the northern plains.

Menlik's right hand went to his sash-girdle and plucked out a carved stick which he waved between them, muttering phrases Travis could not understand. Had the shaman retreated so far along the road to his past that he now believed in his own supernatural powers? Or was this to impress his watching followers?

"You call upon your spirits for aid, Menlik? But the Apache has the companionship of the *ga-n*. Ask of Kaydessa: Who hunts with the Fox in the wilds?" Travis' sharp challenge stopped that wand in mid-air. Menlik's head swung to the girl.

"He hunts with wolves who think like men." She supplied the information the shaman would not openly ask for. "I have seen them act as his scouts. This is no spirit thing, but real and of this world!"

"Any man may train a dog to his bidding!" Menlik spat.

"Does a dog obey orders which are not said aloud? These brown wolves come and sit before him, look into his eyes. And then he knows what lies within their heads, and they know what he would have them do. This is not the way of a master of hounds with his pack!"

Again the murmur ran about the camp as one or two translated. Menlik frowned. Then he rammed his sorcerer's wand back into his sash.

"If you are a man of power—such powers," he said slowly, "then you may walk alone where those who talk with spirits go—into the mountains." He then spoke over his shoulder in his native tongue, and one of the women reached behind her into a hut, brought out a skin bag and a horn cup. Kaydessa took the cup from her and held it while the other woman poured a white liquid from the bag to fill it.

Kaydessa passed the cup to Menlik. He pivoted with it in his hand, dribbling expertly over its brim a few drops at each point of the compass, chanting as he moved. Then he sucked in a mouthful of the contents before presenting the vessel to Travis.

The Apache smelled the same sour scent that had clung to the emptied bag in the foothills. And another part of memory supplied him with the nature of the drink. This was kumiss, a fermented mare's milk which was the wine and water of the steppes.

He forced himself to swallow a draft, though it was alien to his taste, and passed the cup back to Menlik. The shaman emptied the horn and, with that, set aside ceremony. With an upraised hand he beckoned Travis to the fire again, indicating a pot set on the coals.

"Rest . . . eat!" he bade abruptly.

Night was gathering in. Travis tried to calculate how far Tsoay must have backtracked to the rancheria. He thought that he could have already made the pass and be within a day and a half from the Apache camp if he pushed on, as he would. As to where the coyotes were, Travis had no idea. But it was plain that he himself must remain in this encampment for the night or risk rousing the Mongols' suspicion once more.

He ate of the stew, spearing chunks out of the pot with the point of his knife. And it was not until he sat back, his hunger appeased, that the shaman dropped down beside him.

"The Khatun Kaydessa says that when she was slave to the caller, you did not feel its chains," he began.

"Those who rule you are not my overlords. The bonds they set upon your minds do not touch me." Travis hoped that that was the truth and his escape that morning had not been just a fluke.

"This could be, for you and I are not of one blood," Menlik agreed. "Tell me—how did you escape your bonds?"

"The machine which held us so was broken," Travis replied with a portion of the truth, and Menlik sucked in his breath.

"The machines, always the machines!" he cried hoarsely. "A thing which can sit in a man's head and make him do what it will against his will; it is demon sent! There are other machines to be broken, Apache."

"Words will not break them," Travis pointed out.

"Only a fool rides to his death without hope of striking a single blow before he chokes on the blood in his throat," Menlik retorted. "We cannot use bow or tulwar against weapons which flame and kill quicker than any storm lightning! And always the mind machines can make a man drop his knife and stand helplessly waiting for the slave collar to be set on his neck!"

Travis asked a question of his own. "I know that they can bring a caller part way into this mountain, for this very day I saw its effects upon the maiden. But there are many places in the hills well set for ambushes, and those unaffected by the machine could be waiting there. Would there be many machines so that they could send out again and again?"

Menlik's bony hand played with his wand. Then a slow smile curved his lips into the guise of a hunting cat's noiseless snarl.

"There is meat in that pot, Apache, rich meat, good for the filling of a lean belly! So men whose minds the machine could not trouble—such men to be waiting in ambush for the taking of the men who use such a machine—yes. But here would have to be bait, very good bait for such a trap, Lord of Wiles. Never do those others come far into the mountains. Their flyer does not lift well here, and they do not trust traveling on horseback. They were greatly angered to come so far in to reach Kaydessa, though they could not have been too close, or you would not have escaped at all. Yes, strong bait."

"Such bait as perhaps the knowledge that there were strangers across the mountains?"

Menlik turned his wand about in his hands. He

was no longer smiling, and his glance at Travis was sharp and swift.

"Do you sit as Khan in your tribe, Lord?"

"I sit as one they will listen to." Travis hoped that was so. Whether Buck and the moderates would hold clan leadership upon his return was a fact he could not count upon as certain.

"This is a thing which we must hold council over," Menlik continued. "But it is an idea of power. Yes, one to think about, Lord. And I shall think . . ."

He got up and moved away. Travis blinked at the fire. He was very tired, and he disliked sleeping in this camp. But he must not go without the rest his body needed to supply him with a clear head in the morning. And not showing uneasiness might be one way of winning Menlik's confidence.

IX

TRAVIS SETTLED his back against the spire of rock and raised his right hand into the path of the sun, cradling in his palm a disk of glistening metal. Flash . . . flash . . . he made the signal pattern just as his ancestors a hundred years earlier and far across space had used trade mirrors to relay war alerts among the Chiricahua and White Mountain ranges. If Tsoay had returned safely, and if Buck had kept the agreed lookout on that peak a mile or so ahead, then the clan would know that he was coming and with what escort.

He waited now, rubbing the small metal mirror absently on the loose sleeve of his shirt, waiting for a reply. Mirrors were best, not smoke fires which would broadcast too far the presence of men in the hills. Tsoay must have returned. . . .

"What is it that you do?"

Menlik, his shaman's robe pulled up so that his breeches and boots were dark against the golden rock, climbed up beside the Apache. Menlik, Hulagur, and Kaydessa were riding with Travis, offering him one of their small ponies to hurry the trip. He was still regarded warily by the Tatars, but he did not blame them for their cautious attitude.

"Ah—" A flicker of light from the point ahead. One . . . two . . . three flashes, a pause, then two more together. He had been read. Buck had dispatched scouts to meet them, and knowing his people's skill at the business, Travis was certain the Tatars would never suspect their flanking unless the Apaches purposefully revealed themselves. Also the Tatars were not to go to the rancheria, but would be met at a mid-point by a delegation of Apaches. This was no time for the Tatars to learn just how few the clan numbered.

Menlik watched Travis flash an acknowledgment to the sentry ahead. "In this way you speak to your men?"

"This way I speak."

"A thing good and to be remembered. We have the drum, but that is for the ears of all with hearing. This is for the eyes only of those on watch for it. Yes, a good thing. And your people—they will meet with us?"

"They wait ahead," Travis confirmed.

It was close to midday and the heat, gathered in the rocky ways, was like a heaviness in the air itself. The Tatars had shucked their heavy jackets and rolled the fur brims of their hats far up their heads away from their sweat-beaded faces. And at every halt they passed from hand to hand the skin bag of kumiss.

Now even the ponies shuffled on with drooping heads, picking a way in a cut which deepened into a canyon. Travis kept a watch for the scouts. And not for the first time he thought of the disappearance of the coyotes. Somehow, back in the Tatar camp, he had counted confidently on the animals' rejoining him once he had started his return over the mountains.

But he had seen nothing of either beast, nor had he felt that unexplainable mental contact with them which had been present since his first awakening on Topaz. Why they had left him so unceremoniously after defending him from the Mongol attack, and why they were keeping themselves aloof now, he did not know. But he was conscious of a thread of alarm for their continued absence, and he hoped he would find they had gone back to the rancheria.

The ponies thudded dispiritedly along a sandy wash which bottomed the canyon. Here the heat became a leaden weight and the men were panting like four-footed beasts running before hunters. Finally Travis sighted what he had been seeking, a flicker of movement on the wall well above. He flung up his hand, pulling his mount to a stand. Apaches stood in full view, bows ready, arrows on cords. But they made no sound.

Kaydessa cried out, booted her mount to draw equal with Travis.

"A trap!" Her face, flushed with heat, was also stark with anger.

Travis smiled slowly. "Is there a rope about you, Wolf Daughter?" he inquired softly. "Are you now dragged across this sand?"

Her mouth opened and then closed again. The quirt she had half raised to slash at him, flopped across her pony's neck.

The Apache glanced back at the two men. Hulagur's hand was on his sword hilt, his eyes darting from one of those silent watchers to the next. But the utter hopelessness of the Tatar position was too plain. Only Menlik made no move toward any weapon, even his spirit wand. Instead, he sat quietly in the saddle, displaying no emotion toward the Apaches save his usual self-confident detachment.

"We go on." Travis pointed ahead.

Just as suddenly as they had appeared from the heart of the golden cliffs, so did the scouts vanish. Most of them were already on their way to the point Buck had selected for the meeting place. There had been only six men up there, but the Tatars had no way of knowing just how large a portion of the whole clan that number was.

Travis' pony lifted his head, nickered, and achieved a stumbling trot. Somewhere ahead was water, one of those oases of growth and life which pocked the whole mountain range—to the preservation of all animals and all men.

Menlik and Hulagur pushed on until their mounts were hard on the heels of the two ridden by the girl and Travis. Travis wondered if they still waited for some arrow to strike home, though he saw that both men rode with outward disregard for the patrolling scouts.

A grass-leaf bush beckoned them on and again the ponies quickened pace, coming out into a tributary canyon which housed a small pool and a good stand of grass and brush. To one side of the water Buck stood, his arms folded across his chest, armed only with his belt knife. Grouped behind him were Deklay, Tsoay, Nolan, Manulito—Travis tabulated hurriedly. Manulito and Deklay were to be classed together—or had been when he was last in the ran-

cheria. On Buck's stairway from the past, both had
halted more than halfway down. Nolan was a quiet
man who seldom spoke, and whose opinion Travis
could not foretell. Tsoay would back Buck.

Probably such a divided party was the best Travis
could have hoped to gather. A delegation composed
entirely of those who were ready to leave the past of
the Redax—a collection of Bucks and Jil-Lees—was
outside the bounds of possibility. But Travis was
none too happy to have Deklay in on this.

Travis dismounted, letting the pony push forward
by himself to dip nose into the pool.

"This is," Travis pointed politely with his
chin—"Menlik, one who talks with spirits. . . .
Hulagur, who is son to a chief . . . and Kaydessa,
who is daughter to a chief. They are of the horse
people of the north." He made the introduction
carefully in English.

Then he turned to the Tatars. "Buck, Deklay,
Nolan, Manulito, Tsoay," he named them all,
"these stand to listen, and to speak for the
Apaches."

But sometime later when the two parties sat facing
each other, he wondered whether a common decision could come from the clansmen on his side of
that irregular circle. Deklay's expression was
closed; he had even edged a short way back, as if he
had no desire to approach the strangers. And Travis
read into every line of Deklay's body his distrust and
antagonism.

He himself began to speak, retelling his adven-
tures since they had followed Kaydessa's trail,
sketching in the situation at the Tartar-Mongol settlement as he had learned it from her and from

Menlik. He was careful to speak in English so that the Tatars could hear all he was reporting to his own kind. And the Apaches listened blank-faced, though Tsoay must already have reported much of this. When Travis was done it was Deklay who asked a question:

"What have we to do with these people?"

"There is this—" Travis chose his words carefully, thinking of what might move a warrior still conditioned to riding with the raiders of a hundred years earlier, "the Pinda-lick-o-yi (whom we call 'Reds,') are never willing to live side by side with any who are not of their mind. And they have weapons such as make our bow cords bits of rotten string, our knives slivers of rust. They do not kill; they enslave. And when they discover that we live, then they will come against us—"

Deklay's lips moved in a wolf grin. "This is a large land, and we know how to use it. The Pinda-lick-o-yi will not find us—"

"With their eyes maybe not," Travis replied. "With their machines—that is another matter."

"Machines!" Deklay spat. "Always these machines . . . Is that all you can talk about? It would seem that you are bewitched by these machines, which we have not seen—none of us!"

"It was a machine which brought you here," Buck observed. "Go you back and look upon the spaceship and remember, Deklay. The knowledge of the Pinda-lick-o-yi is greater than ours when it deals with metal and wire and things which can be made with both. Machines brought us along the road of the stars, and there is no tracker in the clan who could hope to do the same. But now I have this to ask: Does our brother have a plan?''

"Those who are Reds,'' Travis answered slowly, "they do not number many. But more may later come from our own world. Have you heard of such arriving?'' he asked Menlik.

"Not so, but we are not told much. We live apart and no one of us goes to the ship unless he is summoned. For they have weapons to guard them, or long since they would have been dead. It is not proper for a man to eat from the pot, ride in the wind, sleep easy under the same sky with him who has slain his brother.''

"They have then killed among your people?''

"They have killed,'' Menlik returned briefly.

Kaydessa stirred and muttered a word or two to her brother. Hulagur's head came up, and he exploded into violent speech.

"What does he say?'' Deklay demanded.

The girl replied: "He speaks of our father who aided in the escape of three and so afterward was slain by the leader as a lesson to us—since he was our 'white beard,' the Khan.''

"We have taken the oath in blood—under the Wolf Head Standard—that they will also die,'' Menlik added. "But first we must shake them out of their ship-shell.''

"That is the problem,'' Travis elaborated for the benefit of his clansmen. "We must get these Reds away from their protected camp—out into the open. When they now go they are covered by this 'caller' which keeps the Tatars under their control, but it has no effect on us.''

"So, again I say: What is all this to us?" Deklay got to his feet. "This machine does not hunt us, and we can make our camps in this land where no Pinda-lick-o-yi can find them—"

"We are not *dobe-gusndhe-he*—invulnerable. Nor do we know the full range of machines they can use. It does no one well to say *'doxa-da'*—this is not so—when he does not know all that lies in an enemy's wickiup."

To Travis' relief he saw agreement mirrored on Buck's face, Tsoay's, Nolan's. From the beginning he had had little hope of swaying Deklay; he could only trust that the verdict of the majority would be the accepted one. It went back to the old, old Apache institution of prestige. A *nantan*-chief had the *go'ndi*, the high power, as a gift from birth. Common men could possess horse power or cattle power; they might have the gift of acquiring wealth so they could make generous gifts—be *ikadntl'izi*, the wealthy ones who spoke for their family groups within the loose network of the tribe. But there was no hereditary chieftainship or even an undivided rule within a rancheria. The *nagunlka-dant'an*, or war chief, often led only on the warpath and had no voice in clan matters save those dealing with a raid.

And to have a split now would fatally weaken their small clan. Deklay and those of a like mind might elect to withdraw and not one of the rest could deny him that right.

"We shall think on this," Buck said. "Here is food, water, pasturage for horses, a camp for our visitors. They will wait here." He looked at Travis. "You will wait with them, Fox, since you know their ways."

Travis' immediate reaction was objection, but then he realized Buck's wisdom. To offer the proposition of alliance to the Apaches needed an impartial spokesman. And if he himself did it, Deklay might automatically oppose the idea. Let Buck talk and it would be a statement of fact.

"It is well," Travis agreed.

Buck looked about, as if judging time from the lie of sun and shadow on the ground. "We shall return in the morning when the shadow lies here." With the toe of his high moccasin he made an impression in the soft earth. Then, without any formal farewell, he strode off, the others fast on his heels.

"He is your chief, that one?" Kaydessa asked, pointing after Buck.

"He is one having a large voice in council," Travis replied. He set about building up the cooking fire, bringing out the body of a split-horn calf which had been left them. Menlik sat on his heels by the pool, dipping up drinking water with his hand. Now he squinted his eyes against the probe of the sun.

"It will require much talking to win over the short one," he observed. "That one does not like us or your plan. Just as there will be those among the Horde who will not like it either." He flipped water drops from his fingers. "But this I do know, man who calls himself Fox, if we do not make a common cause, then we have no hope of going against the Reds. It will be for them as a man crushing fleas." He brought his hand down on his knee in emphatic slaps. "So . . . and so . . . and so!"

"This do I think also," Travis admitted.

"So let us both hope that all men will be as wise as we," Menlik said, smiling. "And since we can take a hand in that decision, this remains a time for rest.''

The shaman might be content to sleep the after-noon away, but after he had eaten, Hulagur wan-dered up and down the valley, making a lengthy business of rubbing down their horses with twists of last season's grass. Now and then he paused beside Kaydessa and spoke, his uneasiness plain to Travis although he could not understand the words.

Travis had settled down in the shade, half dozing, yet alert to every movement of the three Tatars. He tried not to think of what might be happening in the rancheria by switching his mind to that misty valley of the towers. Did any of those three alien structures contain such a grab bag of the past as he, Ashe, and Murdock had found on that other world where the winged people had gathered together for them the artifacts of an older civilization? At that time he had created for their hosts a new weapon of defense, turning metal tubes into blow-guns. It had been there, too, where he had chanced upon the library of tapes, one of which had eventually landed Travis and his people here on Topaz.

Even if he did find racks of such tapes in one of those towers, there would be no way of using them—with the ship wrecked on the mountain side. Only—Travis' fingers itched where they lay quiet on his knees—there might be other things waiting. If he were only free to explore!

He reached out to touch Menlik's shoulder. The shaman half turned, opening his eyes with the lan-guid effort of a sleepy cat. But the spark of intelli-gence awoke in them quickly.

''What is it?''

For a moment Travis hesitated, already regretting

his impulse. He did not know how much Menlik remembered of the present. Remember of the present—one part of the Apache's mind was wryly amused at that snarled estimate of their situation. Men who had been dropped into their racial and ancestral pasts until the present time was less real than the dreams conditioning them had a difficult job evaluating any situation. But since Menlik had clung to his knowledge of English, he must be less far down that stairway.

"When we met you, Kaydessa and I, it was outside that valley." Travis was still of two minds about this questioning, but the Tatar camp had been close to the towers and there was a good chance the Mongols had explored them. "And inside were buildings . . . very old . . ."

Menlik was fully alert now. He took his wand, played with it as he spoke:

"That is, or was, a place of much power, Fox. Oh, I know that you question my kinship with the spirits and the powers they give. But one learns not to dispute what one feels here—and here—" His long, somewhat grimy fingers went to his forehead and then to the bare brown chest where his shirt fell open. "I have walked the stone path in that valley, and there have been the whispers—"

"Whispers?"

Menlik twirled the wand. "Whispers which are too low for many ears to distinguish. You can hear them as one hears the buzzing of an insect, but never the words—no, never the words! But that is a place of great power!"

"A place to explore!"

But Menlik watched only his wand. "That I wonder, Fox, truly do I wonder. This is not our world. And here there may be that which does not welcome us.''

Tricks-in-trade of a shaman? Or was it true recognition of something beyond human description? Travis could not be sure, but he knew that he must return to the valley and see for himself.

"Listen," Menlik said, leaning closer, "I have heard your tale, that you were on that first ship, the one which brought you unwilling along the old star paths. Have you ever seen such a thing as this?"

He smoothed a space of soft earth and with the narrow tip of his wand began to draw. Whatever role Menlik had played in the present before he had been reconditioned into a shaman of the Horde, he had had the ability of an artist, for with a minimum of lines he created a figure in that sketch.

It was a man or at least a figure with general human outlines. But the round, slightly oversized skull was bare, the clothing skintight to reveal unnaturally thin limbs. There were large eyes, small nose and mouth, rather crowded into the lower third of the head, giving an impression of an over-expanded brain case above. And it was familiar.

Not the flying men of the other world, certainly not the nocturnal ape-things. Yet for all its alien quality Travis was sure he had seen its like before. He closed his eyes and tried to visualize it apart from lines in the soil.

Such a head, white, almost like the bone of a skull laid bare, such a head lying face down on a bone-thin arm clad in a blue-purple skintight sleeve. Where had he seen it?

The Apache gave a sharp exclamation as he remembered fully. The derelict spaceship as he had first found it—the dead alien officer had still been seated at its controls! The alien who had set the tape which took them out into that forgotten empire —he was the subject of Menlik's drawing!

"Where? When did you see·such a one?" The Apache bent down over the Tatar.

Menlik looked troubled. "He came into my mind when I walked the valley. I thought I could almost see such a face in one of the tower windows, but of that I am not sure. Who is it?"

"Someone from the·old days—those who once ruled the stars," Travis answered. But were they still here then, the remnant of a civilization which had flourished ten thousand years ago? Were the Baldies, who centuries ago had hunted down so ruthlessly the Russians who had dared to loot their wrecked ships, still on Topaz?

He remembered the story of Ross Murdock's escape from those aliens in the far past of Europe, and he shivered. Murdock was tough, steel tough, yet his own description of that epic chase and the final meeting had carried with it his terror. What could a handful of primitively armed and almost primitively minded Terrans do now if they had to dispute Topaz with the Baldies?

X

"BEYOND THIS—" Menlik worked his way to the very lip of a drop, raising a finger cautiously— "beyond this we do not go."

"But you say that the camp of your people lies well out in the plains—" Jil-Lee was up on one knee, using the field glasses they had brought from the stores of the wrecked ship. He passed them along to Travis. There was nothing to be sighted but the rippling amber waves of the tall grasses, save for an occasional break of a copse of trees near the foothills.

They had reached this point in the early morning, threading through the pass, making their way across the section known to the outlaws. From here they could survey the debatable land where their temporary allies insisted the Reds were in full control.

The result of the conference in the south had been this uneasy alliance. From the start Travis realized that he could not hope to commit the clan to any set plan, that even to get this scouting party to come against the stubborn resistance of Deklay and his reactionaries was a major achievement. There was now an opening wedge of six Apaches in the north.

"Beyond this," Menlik repeated, "they keep watch and can control us with the caller."

"What do you think?" Travis passed the glasses to Nolan.

If they were ever to develop a war chief, this lean man, tall for an Apache and slow to speak, might fill that role. He adjusted the lenses and began a detailed study-sweep of the open territory. Then he stiffened; his mouth, below the masking of the glasses, was tight.

"What is it?" Jil-Lee asked.

"Riders—two . . . four . . . five . . . Also something else—in the air."

Menlik jerked back and grabbed at Nolan's arm, dragging him down by the weight of his body.

"The flyer! Come back—back!" He was still pulling at Nolan, prodding at Travis with one foot, and the Apaches stared at him with amazement.

The shaman sputtered in his own language, and then, visibly regaining command of himself, spoke English once more.

"Those are hunters, and they carry a caller. Either some others have escaped or they are determined to find our mountain camp."

Jil-Lee looked at Travis. "You did not feel anything when the woman was under that spell?"

Travis shook his head. Jil-Lee nodded and then said to the shaman: "We shall stay here and watch. But since it is bad for you—do you go. And we shall meet you near this place of the towers. Agreed?"

For a moment Menlik's face held a shadowy expression Travis tried to read. Was it resentment—resentment that he was forced to retreat when the others could stand their ground? Did the Tatar believe that he lost face this way? But the shaman gave a grunt of what they took as assent and slipped over the edge of the lookout point. A moment later they heard him speaking the Mongol tongue, warning Hulagur and Lotchu, his companions on the scout. Then came the clatter of pony hoofs as they rode their mounts away.

The Apaches settled back in the cup, which gave them a wide view over the plains. Soon it was not necessary to use the glasses in order to sight the advancing party of hunters—five riders, four wearing Tatar dress. The fifth had such an odd outline that Travis was reminded of Menlik's sketch of the alien. Under the sharper vision of the glasses he saw that the rider was equipped with a pack strapped between his shoulders and a bulbous helmet covering most of his head. Highly specialized equipment for communication, Travis guessed.

"That is a 'copter up above," Nolan said. "Different shape from ours."

They had been familiar with helicopters back on Terra. Ranchers used them for range inspection, and all of the Apache volunteers had flown in them. But Nolan was correct; this one possessed several unfamiliar features.

"The Tatars say they don't bring those very far into the mountains." Jil-Lee mused. "That could explain their man on horseback; he gets in where they don't fly."

Nolan fingered his bow. "If these Reds depend upon their machine to control what they seek, then they may be taken by surprise—"

"But not yet!" Travis spoke sharply. Nolan frowned at him.

116

Jil-Lee chuckled. "The way is not so dark for us, younger brother, that we need your torch held for our feet!"

Travis swallowed back any retort, accepting the fairness of that rebuke. He had no right to believe that he alone knew the best way of handling the enemy. Biting on the sourness of that realization, he lay quietly with the others, watching the riders enter the foothills perhaps a quarter of a mile to the west.

The helicopter was circling now over the men riding into a cut between two rises. When they were lost to view, the pilot made wider casts, and Travis thought the flyer's crew were probably in communication with the helmeted one of the quintet on the ground.

He stirred. "They are heading for the Tatar camp, just as if they know exactly where it is—"

"That also may be true," Nolan replied. "What do we know of these Tatars? They have freely said that the Reds can hold them in mind ropes when they wish. Already they may be so bound. I say—let us go back to our own country." He added to the decisiveness of that by handing Jil-Lee the glasses and sliding down from their perch.

Travis looked at the other. In a way he could understand the wisdom of Nolan's suggestion. But he was sure that withdrawal now would only postpone trouble. Sooner or later the Apaches would have to stand against the Reds, and if they could do it now while the enemy was occupied with trouble from the Tatars, so much the better.

Jil-Lee was following Nolan. But something in Travis rebelled. He watched the circling helicopter. If it was overhanging the action area of the horsemen, they had either reined in or were searching a relatively small section of the foothills.

Reluctantly Travis descended to the hollow where Jil-Lee stood with Nolan. Tsoay and Lupe and Rope were a little to one side as if the final orders would come from their seniors.

"It would be well," Jil-Lee said slowly, "if we saw what weapons they have. I want a closer look at the equipment of that one in the helmet. Also," he smiled straight at Nolan—"I do not think that they can detect the presence of warriors of the People unless we will it so."

Nolan ran a finger along the curve of his bow, shot a measuring glance right and left at the general contours of the country.

"There is wisdom in what you say, elder brother. Only this is a trail we shall take alone, not allowing the men with fur hats to know where we walk." He looked pointedly in Travis' direction.

"That is wisdom, *Ba'is'a*," Travis promptly replied, giving Nolan the old title accorded the leader of a war party. Travis was grateful for that much of a concession.

They swung into action, heading southeast at an angle which should bring them across the track of the enemy hunting party. The path was theirs at last, only moments after the passing of their quarry. None of the five riders was taking any precautions to cover his trail. Each moved with the confidence of one not having to fear any attack.

From cover the Apaches looked aloft. They could hear the faint hum of the helicopter. It was still circling, Tsoay reported from a higher check point, but those circles remained close over the plains area—the riders had already passed beyond the limits of that aerial sentry.

Three to a side, the Apaches advanced with the trail between them. They were carefully hidden when they caught up with the hunters. The four Tatars were grouped together; the fifth man, heavily burdened by his pack, had climbed from the saddle and was sitting on the ground, his hands busy with a flat plate which covered him from upper chest to belt.

Now that he had a chance to see them closely, Travis noted the lack of expression on the broad Tatar faces. The four men were blank of eye, astride their mounts with no apparent awareness of their present surroundings. Then as one, their hands swung around to the helmeted leader before they dismounted and stood motionless for a long moment in a way which reminded Travis of the coyotes' attitude when they endeavored to pass some message to him. But these men even lacked the signs of thinking intelligence the animals had.

The helmeted man's hand moved across his chest plate, and instantly his followers came into a measure of life. One put his hand to his forehead with an odd, half-dazed gesture. Another half crouched, his lips wrinkling back in a snarl. And the leader, watching him, laughed. Then he snapped an order, his hand poised over his control plate.

One of the four took the horse reins, made the mounts fast to near-by bushes. Then as one they began to walk forward, the Red bringing up the rear several paces behind the nearest Tatar. They were going upslope to the crest of a small ridge.

The Tatar who first reached the crest put his hand

to cup his mouth, sent a ringing cry southward, and the faint "hu-hu-hu" echoed on and on through the hills.

Either Menlik had reached the camp in time, or his people were not to be so easily enticed. For though the hunters waited for a long time, there was no answer to that hail. At last the helmeted man called his captives, bringing them sullenly down to mount and ride again—a move which suited the Apaches.

They could not tell how close was the communication between the rider and the helicopter. And they were still too near the plains to attack unless it was necessary for their own protection. Travis dropped back to join Nolan.

"He controls them by that plate on his chest," he said. "If we would take them, we must get at that—"

"These Tatars use lariats in fighting. Did they not rope you as a calf is roped for branding? Then why do they not so take this Red, binding his arms to his sides?" The suspicion in Nolan's voice was plain.

"Perhaps in them is some conditioned control making it so that they cannot attack their rulers—"

"I do not like this matter of machines which can play this way and that with minds and bodies!" flared Nolan. "A man should only *use* a weapon, not be one!"

Travis could agree to that. Had they by the wreck of their own ship and the death of Ruthven, escaped just such an existence as these Tatars now endured? If so, why? He and all the Apaches were volunteers, eager and willing to form new world colonies. What had happened back on Terra that they had been so ruthlessly sent out without warning and under Redax? Another small piece of that puzzle, or maybe the heart of the whole picture snapped into place. Had the project learned in some way of the Tatar settlement on Topaz and so been forced to speed up that translation from late twentieth-century Americans to primitives? That would explain a lot!

Travis returned abruptly to the matter now at hand as he saw a peak ahead. The party they were trailing was heading directly for the outlaw hide-out. Travis hoped Menlik had warned them in time. There—that wall of cliff to his left must shelter the valley of the towers, though it was still miles ahead. Travis did not believe the hunters would be able to reach their goal unless they traveled at night. They might not know of the ape-things which could menace the dark.

But the enemy, whether he knew of such dangers or not, did not intend to press on. As the sun pulled away, leaving crevices and crannies shadow dark, the hunters stopped to make camp. The Apaches, after their custom on the war trail, gathered on the heights above.

"This Red seems to think that he shall find those he seeks sitting waiting for him, as if their feet were nipped tight in a trap," Tsoay remarked.

"It is the habit of the Pinda-lick-o-yi," Lupe added, "to believe they are greater than all others. Yet this one is a stupid fool walking into the arms of a she-bear with a cub." He chuckled.

"A man with a rifle does not fear a man armed only with a stick," Travis cut in quickly. "This one is armed with a weapon which he has good reason to believe makes him invulnerable to attack. If he rests tonight, he probably leaves his machine on guard."

"At least we are sure of one thing," Nolan said in half agreement. "This one does not suspect that there are any in these hills save those he can master. And his machine does not work against us. Thus at dawn—" He made a swift gesture, and they smiled in concert.

At dawn—the old time of attack. An Apache does not attack at night. Travis was not sure that any of them could break that old taboo and creep down upon the camp before the coming of new light.

But tomorrow morning they would take over this confident Red, strip him of his enslaving machine.

Travis' head jerked. It had come as suddenly as a blow between his eyes—to half stun him. What . . . what was it? Not any physical impact—no, something which was dazing but still immaterial. He braced his whole body, awaiting its return, trying frantically to understand what had happened in that instant of vertigo and seeming disembodiment. Never had he experienced anything like it—or had he? Two years or more ago when he had gone through the time transfer to enter the Arizona of the Folsom Men some ten thousand years earlier—that moment of transfer had been something like this, a sensation of being awry in space and time with no stable footing to be found.

Yet he was lying here on very tangible rock and soil, and nothing about him in the shadow-hung landscape of Topaz had changed in the slightest. But that blow had left behind it a quivering residue of panic buried far inside him, a tender spot like an open wound.

Travis drew a deep breath which was almost a sob, levered himself up on one elbow to stare intently down into the enemy camp. Was this some attack from the other's unknown weapon? Suddenly he was not at all sure what might happen when the Apaches made that dawn rush.

Jil-Lee was in station on his right. Travis must compare notes with him to be sure that this was not indeed a trap. Better to retreat now than to be taken like fish in a net. He crept out of his place, gave the chittering signal call of the fluff-ball, and heard Jil-Lee's answer in a cleverly mimicked trill of a night insect.

"Did you feel something just now—in your head?" Travis found it difficult to put that sensation into words.

"Not so. But you did?"

He had—of course, he had! The remains of it were still in him, that point of panic. "Yes."

"The machine?"

"I don't know." Travis confusion grew. It might be that he alone of the party had been struck. If so, he could be a danger to his own kind.

"This is not good. I think we had better hold council, away from here." Jil-Lee's whisper was the merest ghost of sound. He chirped again to be answered from Tsoay upslope, who passed on the signal.

The first moon was high in the sky as the Apaches gathered together. Again Travis asked his question: Had any of the others felt that odd blow? He was met by negatives.

But Nolan had the final word: "This is not good," he echoed Jil-Lee's comment "If it was the Red machine at work, then we may all be swept into his net along with those he seeks. Perhaps the longer one remains close to that thing, the more influence it gains over him. We shall stay here until dawn. If the enemy would reach the place they seek, then they must pass below us, for that is the easiest road. Burdened with his machine, that Red has ever taken the easiest way. So, we shall see if he also has a defense against these when they come without warning.'' He touched the arrows in his quiver.

To kill from ambush meant that they might never learn the secret of the machine, but after his experience Travis was willing to admit that Nolan's caution was the wise way. Travis wanted no part of a second attack like that which had shaken him so. And Nolan had not ordered a general retreat. It must be in the war chief's thoughts as it was in Travis' that if the machine could have an influence over Apaches, it must cease to function.

They set their ambush with the age-old skill the Redax had grafted into their memories. Then there was nothing to do but wait.

It was an hour after dawn when Tsoay signaled that the enemy was coming, and shortly after, they heard the thud of ponies' hoofs. The first Tatar plodded into view, and by the stance of his body in the saddle, Travis knew the Red had him under full control. Two, then three Tatars passed between the teeth of the Apache trap. The fourth one had allowed a wider gap to open between himself and his fellows.

Then the Red leader came. His face below the bulge of the helmet was not happy. Travis believed the man was not a horseman by inclination. The Apache set arrow to bow cord, and at the chirp from Nolan, fired in concert with his clansmen.

Only one of those arrows found a target. The

Red's pony gave a shrill scream of pain and terror, reared, pawing at the air, toppled back, pinning its shouting rider under it.

The Red had had a defense right enough, one which had somehow deflected the arrows. But he neither had protection which had seriously wounded the now threshing pony.

Ahead the Tatars twisted and writhed, mouthed tortured cries, then dropped out of their saddles to lie limply on the ground as if the arrows aimed at the master had instead struck each to the heart.

XI

EITHER THE RED was lucky, or his reactions were quick. He had somehow rolled clear of the struggling horse as Lupe leaped from behind a boulder, knife out and ready. To the eyes of the Apaches the helmeted man lay easy prey to Lupe's attack. Nor did he raise an arm to defend himself, though one hand lay free across the plate on his chest.

But the young Apache stumbled, rebounding back as if he had run into an unseen wall—when his knife was still six inches away from the other. Lupe cried out, shook under a second impact as the Red fired an automatic with his other hand.

Travis dropped his bow, returned to the most primitive weapon of all. His hand closed around a stone and he hurled the fist-sized oval straight at the helmet so clearly outlined against the rocks below.

But even as Lupe's knife had never touched flesh, so was the rock deflected; the Red was covered by some protective field. This was certainly nothing the Apaches had seen before. Nolan's whistle summoned them to draw back.

The Red fired again, the sharp bark of the hand gun harsh and loud. He did not have any real target, for with the exception of Lupe the Apaches had gone to earth. Between the rocks the Red was struggling to his feet, but he moved slowly, favoring his side and one leg; he had not come totally unharmed from his tumble with the pony.

An armed enemy who could not be touched—one who knew there were more than outlaws in this region. The Red leader was far more of a threat to the Apaches now than he had ever been. He must not be allowed to escape.

He was holstering his gun, moving along with one hand against the rocks to steady himself, trying to reach one of the ponies that stood with trailing reins beside the inert Tatars.

But when the enemy reached the far side of that rock he would have to sacrifice either his steadying hold, or his touch on the chest plate where his other hand rested. Would he, then, for an instant be vulnerable?

The pony!

Travis put an arrow on bow cord and shot. Not at the Red, who had released his hold of the rock, preferring to totter instead of lose control of the chest plate—but into the air straight before the nose of the mount.

The pony neighed wildly, tried to turn, and its shoulder caught the free, groping hand of the Red and spun the man around and back, so that he flung up both hands in an effort to ward himself off the rocks. Then the pony stampeded down the break, its companions catching the same fever, trailing in a mad dash which kept the Red hard against the boulders.

He continued to stand there until the horses, save for the wounded one still kicking fruitlessly, were gone. Travis felt a sense of reprieve. They might not be able to get at the Red, but he was hurt and afoot, two strikes which might yet reduce him to a condition the Apaches could handle.

Apparently the other was also aware of that, for now he pushed out from the rocks and stumbled along after the ponies. But he went only a step or two. Then, settling back once more against a convenient boulder, he began to work at the plate on his chest.

Nolan appeared noiselessly beside Travis. "What does he do?" His lips were very close to the younger man's ear, his voice hardly more than a breath.

Travis shook his head slightly. The Red's actions were a complete mystery. Unless, now disabled and afoot, he was trying to summon aid. Though there was no landing place for a helicopter here.

Now was the time to try and reach Lupe. Travis had seen a slight movement in the fallen Apache's hand, the first indication that the enemy's shot had not been as fatal as it had looked. He touched Nolan's arm, pointed to Lupe; and then, discarding his bow and quiver beside the war leader, he stripped for action. There was cover down to the wounded Apache which would aid him. He must pass one of the Tatars on the way, but none of the tribesmen had shown any signs of life since they had fallen from their saddles at the first attack.

With infinite care, Travis lowered himself into a narrow passage, took a lizard's way between brush and boulder, pausing only when he reached the Tatar for a quick check on the potential enemy.

The lean brown face was half turned, one cheek in the sand, but the slack mouth, the closed eyes were those, Travis believed, of a dead man. By some action of his diabolic machine the Red must have snuffed out his four captives—perhaps in the belief that they were part of the Apache attack.

Travis reached the rock where Lupe lay. He knew that Nolan was watching the Red and would give him warning if he suddenly showed an interest in anything but his machine. The Apache reached out, his hands closing on Lupe's ankles. Beneath his touch, flesh and muscle tensed. Lupe's eyes were open, focused now on Travis. There was a bleeding furrow above his right ear. The Red had tried a difficult head shot, failing in his aim by a mere fraction of an inch.

Lupe made a swift move for which Travis was ready. His grip on the other's body helped to tumble them both around a rock which lay between them and the Red. There was the crack of another shot and dust spurted from the side of the boulder. But they lay together, safe for the present, as Travis was sure the enemy would not risk an open attack on their small fortress.

With Travis' aid Lupe struggled back up to the site where Nolan waited. Jil-Lee was there to make competent examination of the boy's wound.

"Creased," he reported. "A sore head, but no great damage. Perhaps a scar later, warrior!" He gave Lupe an encouraging thump on the shoulder, before plastering an aid pack over the cut.

"Now we go!" Nolan spoke with emphatic decision.

"He saw enough of us to know we are not Tatars."

Nolan's eyes were cold, his mouth grim as he faced Travis.

"And how can we fight him—?"

"There is a wall—a wall you cannot see—about

him,'' Lupe broke in. ''When I would strike at him, I could not!''

''A man with invisible protection and a gun,'' Jil-Lee took up the argument. ''How would you deal with him, younger brother?''

''I don't know,'' Travis admitted. Yet he also believed that if they withdrew, left the Red here to be found by his own people, the enemy would immediately begin an investigation of the southern country. Perhaps, pushed by their need for learning more about the Apaches, they would bring the helicopter in over the mountains. The answer to all Apache dangers, for now, lay in the immediate future of this one man.

''He is hurt, he cannot go far on foot. And even if he calls the 'copter, there is no landing place. He will have to move elsewhere to be picked up.'' Travis thought aloud, citing the thin handful of points in their favor.

Tsoay nodded toward the rim of the ravine. ''Rocks up there and rocks can roll. Start an earth-slide . . .''

Something within Travis balked at that. From the first he had been willing enough to slug it out with the Red, weapon to weapon, man to man. Also, he had wanted to take a captive, not stand over a body. But to use the nature of the country against the enemy, that was the oldest Apache trick of all and one they would have to be forced to employ.

Nolan had already nodded in assent, and Tsoay and Jil-Lee started off. Even if the Red did possess a protective wall device, could it operate in full against a landslide? They all doubted that.

The Apaches reached the cliff rim without exposing themselves to the enemy's fire. The Red still sat there calmly, his back against the rock, his hands busy with his equipment as if he had all the time in the world.

Then suddenly came a scream from more than one throat.

"Dar-u-gar!" The ancient war cry of the Mongol Hordes.

Then over the lip of the other slope rose a wave of men—their curved swords out, a glazed set to their eyes—heading for the Ameridians with utter disregard for any personal safety. Menlik in the lead, his shaman's robe flapping wide below his belt like the wings of some oversized predatory bird. Hulagur . . . Jagatai . . . men from the outlaws' camp. And they were not striving to destroy their disabled overlord in the vale below, but to wipe out the Apaches!

Only the fact that the Apaches were already sheltered behind the rocks they were laboring to dislodge gave them a precious few moments of grace. There was no time to use their bows. They could only use knives to meet the swords of the Tatars, knives and the fact that they could fight with unclouded minds.

"He has them under control!" Travis pawed at Jil-Lee's shoulder. "Get him—they'll stop!"

He did not wait to see if the other Apache understood. Instead, he threw the full force of his own body against the rock they had made the center stone of their slide. It gave, rolled, carrying with it and before it the rest of the piled rubble. Travis stumbled, fell flat, and then a body thudded down upon him, and he was fighting for his life to keep a blade from his throat. Around him were the shouts and cries of embroiled warriors; then all was silenced by a roar from below.

Glazed eyes in a face only a foot from his own, the

twisted, panting mouth sending gusts of breath into his nostrils. Suddenly there was reason back in those eyes, a bewilderment which became fear . . . panic . . . The Tatar's body twisted in Travis' hold, striving now not to attack, but to win free. As the Apache loosened his grip the other jerked away, so that for a moment or two they lay gasping, side by side.

Men sat up to look at men. There was a spreading stain down Jil-Lee's side and one of the Tatars sprawled near him, both his hands on his chest, coughing violently.

Menlik clawed at the trunk of a wind-twisted mountain tree, pulled himself to his feet, and stood swaying as might a man long ill and recovering from severe exertion.

Insensibly both sides drew apart, leaving a space between Tatar and Apache. The faces of the Amerindians were grim, those of the Mongols bewildered and then harsh as they eyed their late opponents with dawning reason. What had begun in compulsion for the Tatars might well flare now into rational combat—and from that to a campaign of extermination.

Travis was on his feet. He looked over the lip of the drop. The Red was still in his place down there, a pile of rubble about him. His protection must have failed, for his head was back at an unnatural angle and the dent in his helmet could be easily seen.

"That one is dead—or helpless!" Travis cried out. "Do you still wish to fight for him, Shaman?"

Menlik came away from the tree and walked to the edge of the drop. The others, too, were moving forward. After the shaman looked down he stooped, picked up a small stone, and flung it at the motionless Red. There was a crack of sound. They all saw the tiny spurt of flame, a curl of smoke from the plate on the Red's chest. Not only the man, but his control was finished now.

A wolfish growl and two of the Tatars swung over, started down to the Red. Menlik shouted and they slackened pace.

"We want that," he cried in English. "Perhaps so we can learn—"

"The learning is yours," Jil-Lee replied. "Just as this land is yours, Shaman. But I warn you, from this day do not ride south!"

Menlik turned, the charms on his belt clicking. "So that is the way it is to be, Apache?"

"That is the way it shall be, Tatar! We do not ride to war with allies who may turn their knives against our backs because they are slaves to a machine the enemy controls."

The Tatar's long, slender-fingered hands opened and closed. "You are a wise man, Apache, but sometimes more than wisdom alone is needed—"

"We are wise men, Shaman, let it rest there," Jil-Lee replied somberly.

Already the Apaches were on their way, putting two cliff ridges behind them before they halted to examine and cover their wounds.

"We go." Nolan's chin lifted, indicating the southern route. "Here we do not come again; there is too much witchcraft in this place."

Travis stirred, saw that Jil-Lee was frowning at him.

"Go—?" he repeated.

"Yes, younger brother? You would continue to run with these who are governed by a machine?"

"No. Only, eyes are needed on this side of the mountains."

"Why?" This time Jil-Lee was plainly on the side of the conservatives. "We have now seen this machine at work. It is fortunate that the Red is dead. He will carry no tales of us back to his people as you feared. Thus, if we remain south from now on, we are safe. And this fight between Tatar and Red is none of ours. What do you seek here?"

"I must go again to the place of the towers," Travis answering with the truth. But his friends were facing him with heavy disapproval—now a full row of Deklays.

"Did you not tell us that you felt this strange thing during the night we waited about the camp? What if you become one with these Tatars and are also controlled by the machine? Then you, too, can be made into a weapon against us—your clansmen!" Jil-Lee was almost openly hostile.

Sense was on his side. But in Travis was this other desire of which he was becoming more conscious by the minute. There was a reason for those towers, perhaps a reason important enough for him to discover and run the risk of angering his own people.

"There may be this—" Nolan's voice was remote and cold, "you may already be a piece of this thing, bound to the machines. If so, we do not want you among us."

There it was—an open hostility with more power behind it than Deklay's motiveless disapproval had carried. Travis was troubled. The family, the clan— they were important. If he took the wrong step now and was outlawed from that tight fortress, then as an Apache he would indeed be a lost man. In the past of his people there had been renegades from the tribe—men such as the infamous Apache Kid who had killed and killed again, not only white men but his own people. Wolf men living wolves' lives in the hills. Travis was threatened with that. Yet—up the ladder of civilization, down the ladder—why did this feverish curiosity ride him so cruelly now?

Listen,'' Jil-Lee, his side padded with bandages, stepped closer—''and tell me, younger brother, what is it that you seek in these towers?''

''On another world there were secrets of the old ones to be found in such ancient buildings. Here that might also be true.''

''And among the secrets of those old ones,'' Nolan's voice was still harsh—''were those which brought us to this world, is that not so?''

''Did any man drive you, Nolan, or you, Tsoay, or you Jil-Lee, or any of us, to promise to go beyond the stars? You were told what might be done, and you were eager to try it. You were all volunteers!''

''Save for this voyage when we were told nothing,'' Jil-Lee answered, cutting straight to the heart of the matter. ''Yet, Nolan, I do not believe that it is for more voyage tapes that our youngest brother now searches, nor would those do us any good—as our ship will not rise again from here. What is it that you do seek?''

''Knowledge—weapons, maybe. Can we stand against these machines of the Reds? Yet many of the devices they now use are taken from the star ships they have looted through time. To every weapon there is a defense.''

Nolan blinked and for the first time a hint of interest touched the mask of his face. ''To the bow, the rifle,'' he said softly, ''to the rifle, the machine gun, to the cannon, the big bomb. The defense can be far worse than the first weapon. So you think that in these towers there may be things which shall be to the Reds' machines as the bomb is to the cannon of the Horse Soldiers?''

Travis had an inspiration. "Did not our people lay aside the bow for the rifle when we went up against the Bluecoats?''

"We do not so go up against these Reds!'' protested Lupe.

"Not now. But what if they come across the mountains, perhaps driving the Tatars before them to do their fighting—?''

"And you believe that if you find weapons in these towers, you will know how to use them?'' Jil-Lee asked. "What will give you that knowledge, younger brother?''

"I do not claim such knowledge,'' Travis countered. "But this much I do have: Once I studied to be an archaeologist and I have seen other storehouses of these star people. Who else among us can say as much as that?''

"That is the truth,'' Jil-Lee acknowledged. "Also there is good sense in this seeking out of the tower things. Let the Reds find such first—if they exist at all—and then we may truly be caught in a box canyon with only death at our heels.''

"And you would go to these towers now?'' Nolan demanded.

"I can cut across country and then rejoin you on the other side of the pass!'' The feeling of urgency which had been mounting in Travis was now so demanding that he wanted to race ahead through the wilderness. He was surprised when Jil-Lee put out his palm up as if to warn the younger man.

"Take care, younger brother! This is not a lucky business. And remember, if one goes too far down a wrong trail, there is sometimes no returning—"

"We shall wait on the other side of the pass for one day," Nolan added. "Then—" he shrugged— "where you go will be your own affair."

Travis did not understand that promise of trouble. He was already two steps down his chosen path.

XII

TRAVIS HAD taken a direct cross route through the heights, but not swiftly enough to reach his objective before nightfall. And he had no wish to enter the tower valley by moonlight. In him two emotions now warred. There was the urge to invade the towers, to discover their secret, and flaring higher and higher the beginnings of a new fear. Was he now a battlefield for the superstitions of his race reborn by the Redax and his modern education in the Pinda-lick-o-yi world—half Apache brave of the past, half modern archaeologist with a thirst for knowledge? Or was the fear rooted more deeply and for another reason?

Travis crouched in a hollow, trying to understand what he felt. Why was it suddenly so overwhelmingly important for him to investigate the towers? If he only had the coyotes with him. . . . Why and where had they gone?

He was alive to every noise out of the night, every scent the wind carried to him. The night had its own life, just as the daylight hours held theirs. Only a few of those sounds could he identify, even less did he see. There was one wide-winged, huge flying thing which passed across the green-gold plate of the nearer moon. It was so large that for an instant Travis believed the helicopter had come. Then the wings flapped, breaking the glide, and the creature merged in the shadows of the night—a hunter large enough to be a serious threat, and one he had never seen before.

Relying on his own small defense, the strewing of brittle sticks along the only approach to the hollow, Travis dozed at intervals, his head down on his forearm across his bent knees. But the cold cramped him and he was glad to see the graying sky of pre-dawn. He swallowed two ration tablets and a couple of mouthfuls of water from his canteen and started on.

By sunup he had reached the ledge of the waterfall, and he hurried along the ancient road at a pace which increased to a run the closer he drew to the valley. Deliberately he slowed, his native caution now in control, so that he was walking as he passed through the gateway into the swirling mists which alternately exposed and veiled the towers.

There was no change in the scene from the time he had come there with Kaydessa. But now, rising from a comfortable sprawl on the yellow-and-green pavement, was a welcoming committee— Nalik'ideyu and Naginlta showing no more excitement at his coming than if they had parted only moments before.

Travis went down on one knee, holding out his hand to the female, who had always been the more friendly. She advanced a step or two, touched a cold nose to his knuckles, and whined.

''Why?'' He voiced that one word, but behind it

was a long list of questions. Why had they left him? Why were they here where there was no hunting? Why did they meet him now as if they had calmly expected his return?

Travis glanced from the animals to the towers, those windows set in diamond pattern. And again he was visited by the impression that he was under observation. With the mist floating across those openings, it would be easy for a lurker to watch him unseen.

He walked slowly on into the valley, his mocca-sins making no sound on the pavement, but he could hear the faint click of the coyotes' claws as they paced beside him, on each hand. The sun did not penetrate here, making merely a gilt fog of the first tower, it seemed to Travis that the mist was curling about him; he could no longer see the archway through which he had entered the valley.

"Naye'nezyani—Slayer of Monsters—give strength to the bow arm, to the knife wrist!" Out of what long-buried memory did that ancient plea come? Travis was hardly aware of the sense of the words until he spoke them aloud. "You who wait—*shi- inday to-day ishan*—an Apache is not food for you! I am Fox of the Itcatcudnde'yu—the Eagle People; and beside me walk *ga'ns* of power . . ."

Travis blinked and shook his head as one waking. Why had he spoken so, using words and phrases which were not part of any modern speech?

He moved on, around the base of the first tower, to find no door, no break in its surface below the second-story windows—to the next structure and the next, until he had encircled all three. If he were to enter any, he must find a way of reaching the lowest windows.

On he went to the other opening of the valley, the one which gave upon the territory of the Tatar camp. But he did not sight any of the Mongols as he hacked down a sapling, trimmed, and smoothed it into a blunt-pointed lance. His sash-belt, torn into even strips and knotted together, gave him a rope which he judged would be barely long enough for is purpose.

Then Travis made a chancy cast for the lower window of the nearest tower. On the second try the lance slipped in, and he gave a quick jerk, jamming the lance as a bar across the opening. It was a frail ladder but the best he could improvise. He climbed until the sill of the window was within reach and he could pull himself up and over.

The sill was a wide one, at least a twenty-four-inch span between the inner and outer surface of the tower. Travis sat there for a minute, reluctant to enter. Near the end of his dangling scarf-rope the two coyotes lay on the pavement, their heads up, their tongues lolling from their mouths, their expressions ones of detached interest.

Perhaps it was the width of the outer wall that subdued the amount of light in the room. The chamber was circular, and directly opposite him was a second window, the lowest of the matching diamond pattern. He took the four-foot drop from the sill to the floor but lingered in the light as he surveyed every inch of the room. There were no furnishings at all, but in the very center sank a well of darkness. A smooth pillar, glowing faintly, rose from its core. Travis' adjusting eyes noted how the light came in small ripples-green and purple, over a foundation shade of dark blue.

The pillar seemed rooted below and it extended up through a similar opening in the ceiling, providing the only possible exit up or down, save for climbing from window to window outside. Travis moved slowly to the well. Underfoot was a smooth surface overlaid with a velvet carpet of dust which arose in languid puffs as he walked. Here and there he sighted prints in the dust, strange triangular wedges which he thought might possibly have been made by the claws of birds. But there were no other footprints. This tower had been undisturbed for a long, long time.

He came to the well and looked down. There was dark there, dark in which the pulsations of light from the pillar shone the stronger. But that glow did not extend beyond the edge of the well through which the thick rod threaded. Even by close examination he could detect no break in the smooth surface of the pillar, nothing remotely resembling hand- or footholds. If it did serve the purpose of a staircase, there were no treads.

At last Travis put out his hand to touch the surface of the pillar. And then he jerked back—to no effect. There was no breaking contact between his fingers and an unknown material which had the sleekness of polished metal but—and the thought made him slightly queasy—the warmth and very slight give of flesh!

He summoned all his strength to pull free and could not. Not only did that hold grip him, but his other hand and arm were being drawn to join the first! Inside Travis primitive fears awoke full force, and he threw back his head, voicing a cry of panic as wild as that of a hunting beast.

An instant later, his left palm was as tight a prisoner as his right. And with both hands so held, his whole body was suddenly snapped forward, off the safe foundation of the floor, tight to the pillar.

In this position he was sucked down into the well. And while unable to free himself from the pillar, he did slip along its length easily enough. Travis shut his eyes in an involuntary protest against this weird form of capture, and a shiver ran through his body as he continued to descend.

After the first shock had subsided the Apache realized that he was not truly falling at all. Had the pillar been horizontal instead of vertical, he would have gauged its speed that of a walk. He passed through two more room enclosures; he must already be below the level of the valley floor outside. And he was still a prisoner of the pillar, now in total darkness.

His feet came down against a level surface, and he guessed he must have reached the end. Again he pulled back, arching his shoulders in a final desperate attempt at escape, and stumbled away as he was released.

He came up sideways against a wall and stood there panting. The light, which might have come from the pillar but which seemed more a part of the very air was bright enough to reveal that he was in a corridor running into greater dark both right and left.

Travis took two strides back to the pillar, fitted his palms once again to its surface, with no result. This time his flesh did not adhere and there was no possible way for him to climb that slick pole. He could only hope that at some point the corridor would give him access to the surface. But which way to go—?

At last he chose the right-hand path and started along it, pausing every few steps to listen. But there was no sound except the soft pad of his own feet. The air was fresh enough, and he thought he could detect a faint current coming toward him from some point ahead—perhaps an exit.

Instead, he came into a room and a small gasp of astonishment was wrung out of him. The walls were blank, covered with the same ripples of blue-purple-green light which colored the pillar. Just before him was a table and behind it a bench, both carved from the native yellow-red mountain rock. And there was no exit except the doorway in which he now stood.

Travis walked to the bench. Immovable, it was placed so that whoever sat there must face the opposite wall of the chamber with the table before him. And on the table was an object Travis recognized immediately from his voyage in the alien star ship, one of the reader-viewers through which the involuntary explorers had learned what little they knew of the older galactic civilization.

A reader—and beside it a box of tapes. Travis touched the edge of that box gingerly, half expecting it to crumble into nothingness. This was a place long deserted. Stone table, bench, the towers could survive through centuries of abandonment, but these other objects . . .

The substance of the reader was firm under the film of dust; there was less dust here than had been in the upper tower chamber. Hardly knowing why,

Travis threw one leg over the bench and sat down behind the table, the reader before him, the box of tapes just beyond his hand.

He surveyed the walls and then looked away hurriedly. The rippling colors caught at his eyes. He had a feeling that if he watched that ebb and flow too long, he would be captured in some subtle web of enchantment just as the Reds' machine had caught and held the Tatars. He turned his attention to the reader. It was, he believed, much like the one they had used on the ship.

This room, table, bench, had all been designed with a set purpose. And that purpose—Travis' fingers rested on the box of tapes he could not yet bring himself to open—that purpose was to use the reader, he would swear to that. Tapes so left must have had a great importance for those who left them. It was as if the whole valley was a trap to channel a stranger into this underground chamber.

Travis snapped open the box, fed the first disk into the reader, and applied his eyes to the vision tube at its apex.

The rippling walls looked just the same when he looked up once more, but the cramp in his muscles told Travis that time had passed—perhaps hours instead of minutes—since he had taken out the first disk. He cupped his hands over his eyes and tried to think clearly. There had been sheets of meaningless symbol writing, but also there had been many clear, three-dimensional pictures, accompanied by a singsong commentary in an alien tongue, seemingly voiced out of thin air. He had been stuffed with ragged bits and patches of information, to be connected only by guesses, and some wild guesses, too.

But this much he did know—these towers had been built by the bald spacemen, and they were highly important to that vanished stellar civilization. The information in this room, as disjointed as it had been for him, led to a treasure trove on Topaz greater than he had dreamed.

Travis swayed on the bench. To know so much and yet so little! If Ashe were only here, or some other of the project technicians! A treasure such as Pandora's box had been peril for one who opened it and did not understand. The Apache studied the three walls of blue-purple-green in turn and with new attention. There were ways through those walls; he was fairly sure he could unlock at least one of them. But not now—certainly not now!

And there was another thing he knew: The Reds must *not* find this. Such a discovery on their part would not only mean the end of his own people on Topaz, but the end of Terra as well. This could be a new and alien Black Death spread to destroy whole nations at a time!

If he could—much as his archaeologist's training would argue against it—he would blot out this whole valley above and below ground. But while the Reds might possess a means of such destruction, the Apaches did not. No, he and his people must prevent its discovery by the enemy by doing what he had seen as necessary from the first—wiping out the Red leaders! And that must be done before they chanced upon the towers!

Travis arose stiffly. His eyes ached, his head felt stuffed with pictures, hints, speculations. He wanted to get out, back into the open air where perhaps the clean winds of the heights would blow some of this frightening half knowledge from his benumbed mind. He lurched down the corridor, puzzled now by the problem of getting back to the window level.

Here, before him, was the pillar. Without hope, but still obeying some buried instinct, Travis again set his hands to its surface. There was a tug at his cramped arms; once more his body was sucked to the pillar. This time he was rising!

He held his breath past the first level and then relaxed. The principle of this weird form of transportation was entirely beyond his understanding, but as long as it worked in reverse he didn't care to find out. He reached the windowed chamber, but the sunlight had left it; instead, the clean cut of moon sweep lay on the dusty floor. He must have been hours in that underground place.

Travis pulled away from the embrace of the pillar. The bar of his wooden lance was still across the window and he ran for it. To catch the scouting party at the pass he must hurry. The report they would make to the clan now had to be changed radically in the face of his new discoveries. The Apaches dared not retreat southward and withdraw from the fight, leaving the Reds to use what treasure lay here.

As he hit the pavement below he looked about for the coyotes. Then he tried the mind call. But as mysteriously as they had met him in the valley, so now were they gone again. And Travis had no time to hunt for them. With a sigh, he began his race to the pass.

In the old days, Travis remembered, Apache warriors had been able to cover forty-five or fifty miles a day on foot and over rough territory. But perhaps his modern breeding had slowed him. He had been so sure he could catch up before the others were through the pass. But he stood now in the hollow where they had camped, read the sign of overturned stone and bent twig left for him, and knew they would reach the rancheria and report the decision Deklay and the others wanted before he could head them off.

Travis slogged on. He was so tired now that only the drug from the sustenance tablets he mouthed at intervals kept him going at a dogged pace, hardly more than a swift walk. And always his mind was haunted by fragments of pictures, pictures he had seen in the reader. The big bomb had been the nightmare of his own world for so long, and what was that against the forces the bald star rovers had been able to command?

He fell beside a stream and slept. There was sunshine about him as he arose to stagger on. What day was this? How long had he sat in the tower chamber? He was not sure of time any more. He only knew that he must reach the rancheria, tell his story, somehow win over Deklay and the other reactionaries to prove the necessity for invading the north in force.

A rocky point which was a familiar landmark came into focus. He padded on, his chest heaving, his breath whistling through parched, sun-cracked lips. He did not know that his face was now a mask of driven resolution.

"Hahhhhhh—"

The cry reached his dulled ears. Travis lifted his head, saw the men before him and tried to think what that show of weapons turned toward him could mean.

A stone thudded to earth only inches before his

feet, to be followed by another. He wavered to a stop.

"*Ni'ilgac—!*"

Witch? Where was a witch? Travis shook his head. There was no witch.

"*Do ne'ilka da'!*"

The old death threat, but why—for whom?

Another stone, this one hitting him in the ribs with force enough to send him reeling back and down. He tried to get up again, saw Deklay grin widely and take aim—and at last Travis realized what was happening.

Then there was a bursting pain in his head and he was falling—falling into a well of black, this time with no pillar of blue to guide him.

XIII

THE RASP of something wet and rough, persistent against his cheek; Travis tried to turn his head to avoid the contact and was answered by a burst of pain which trailed off into a giddiness, making him fear another move, no matter how minor. He opened his eyes and saw the pointed ears, the outline of a coyote head between him and a dull gray sky, was able to recognize Nalik'ideyu.

A wetness other than that from the coyote's tongue slid down his forehead now. The dull clouds overhead had released the first heavy rain Travis had experienced since their landing on Topaz. He shivered as the chill damp of his clothes made him aware that he must have been lying out in the full force of the downpour for some time.

It was a struggle to get to his knees, but Nalik'ideyu mouthed a hold on his shirt, tugging and pulling so that somehow he crept into a hollow beneath the branches of a tree where the spouting water was lessened to a few pattering drops.

There the Apache's strength deserted him again and he could only hunch over, his bent knees against his chest trying to endure the throbbing misery in his head, the awful floating sensation which followed any movement. Fighting against that, he tried to remember just what had happened.

The meeting with Deklay and at least four or five others . . . then the Apache accusation of witchcraft, a serious thing in the old days. Old days! To Deklay and his fellows, these *were* the old days! And the threat that Deklay or some other had shouted at him—"*Do ne' ilka da'* "—meant literally: "It won't dawn for you—death!"

Stones, the last thing Travis remembered were the stones. Slowly his hands went out to explore his body. There was more than one bruised area on his shoulders and ribs, even on his thighs. He must still have been a target after he had fallen under the stones which had knocked him unconscious. Stones . . . outlawed! But why? Surely Deklay's hostility could not have swept Buck, Jil-Lee, Tsoay, even Nolan, into agreeing to that? Now he could not think straight.

Travis became aware of warmth, not only of warmth and the soft touch of a furred body by his side, but a comforting communication of mind, a feeling he had no words to describe adequately. Nalik'ideyu was sitting crowded against him, her nose thrust up to rest on his shoulder. She breathed in soft puffs which stirred the loose locks of his rain-damp hair. And now he flung one arm about her, a gesture which brought a whisper of answering whine.

He was past wondering about the actions of the coyotes, only supremely thankful for Nalik'ideyu's present companionship. And a moment later when her mate squeezed under the low loop of a branch and joined them in this natural wickiup, Travis held out his other hand, drew it lovingly across Naginlta's wet hide.

"Now what?" he asked aloud. Deklay could only

have taken such a drastic action with the majority of the clan solidly behind him. It could well be that this reactionary was the new chief, this act of Travis' expulsion merely adding to Deklay's growing prestige.

The shivering which had begun when Travis recovered consciousness, still shook him at intervals. Back on Terra, like all the others in the team, he had had every inoculation known to the space physicians, including several experimental ones. But the cold virus could still practically immobilize a man, and this was no time to give body room to chills and fever.

Catching his breath as his movements touched to life the pain in one bruise after another, Travis peeled off his soaked clothing, rubbed his body dry with handfuls of last year's leaves culled from the thick carpet under him, knowing there was nothing he could do until the whirling in his head disappeared. So he burrowed into the leaves until only his head was uncovered, and tried to sleep, the coyotes curling up one on either side of his nest.

He dreamed but later could not remember any incident from those dreams, save a certain frustration and fear. When he awoke, again to the sound of steady rain, it was dark. He reached out—both coyotes were gone. His head was clearer and suddenly he knew what must be done. As soon as his body was strong enough, he, too, would return to instincts and customs of the past. This situation was desperate enough for him to challenge Deklay.

In the dark Travis frowned. He was slightly taller, and three or four years younger than his enemy. But Deklay had the advantage in a stouter build and longer reach. However, Travis was sure that in his present life Deklay had never fought a duel—Apache fashion. And an Apache duel was not a meeting anyone entered into lightly. Travis had the right to enter the rancheria and deliver such a challenge. Then Deklay must meet him or admit himself in the wrong. That part of it was simple.

But in the past such duels had just one end, a fatal one for at least one of the fighters. If Travis took this trail, he must be prepared to go the limit. And he didn't want to kill Deklay! There were too few of them here on Topaz to make any loss less than a real catastrophe. While he had no liking for Deklay, neither did he nurse any hatred. However, he must challenge the other or remain a tribal outcast; and Travis had no right to gamble with time and the future, not after what he had learned in the tower. It might be his life and skill, or Deklay's against the blotting out of them all—and their home world into the bargain.

First, he must locate the present camp of the clan. If Nolan's arguments had counted, they would be heading south away from the pass. And to follow would draw him farther from the tower valley. Travis' battered face ached as he grinned bitterly. This was another time when a man could wish he were two people, a scout on sentry duty at the valley, the fighter heading in the opposite direction to have it out with Deklay. But since he was merely one man he would have to gamble on time, one of the trickiest risks of all.

Before dawn Nalik'ideyu returned, carrying with her a bird—or at least birds must have been somewhere in the creature's ancestry, but the present representative of its kind had only vestigial remnants of wings, its trailing feet and legs well developed and far more powerful.

Travis skinned the corpse, automatically putting aside some spine quills to feather future arrows. Then he ate slivers of dusky meat raw, throwing the bones to Nalik'ideyu.

Though he was still stiff and sore, Travis was determined to be on his way. He tried mind contact with the coyote, picturing the Apaches, notably Deklay, as sharply as he could by mental image. And her assent was clear in return. She and her mate were willing to lead him to the tribe. He gave a slight sigh of relief.

As he slogged on through the depressing drizzle, the Apache wondered again why the coyotes had left him before and waited in the tower valley. What link was there between the animals of Terra and the reamins of the long-ago empire of the stars? For he was certain it was not by chance that Nalik'ideyu and Naginlta had lingered in that misty place. He longed to communicate with them directly, to ask questions and be answered.

Without their aid, Travis would never have been able to track the clan. The drizzle alternated with slashing bursts of rain, torrential enough to drive the trackers to the nearest cover. Overhead the sky was either dull bronze or night black. Even the coyotes paced nose to ground, often making wide casts for the trail while Travis waited.

The rain lasted for three days and nights, filling water-courses with rapidly rising streams. Travis could only hope that the others were having the same difficulty traveling that he was, perhaps the more so since they were burdened with packs. The fact that they kept on meant that they were determined to get as far from the northern mountains as they could.

On the fourth morning the bronze of the clouds slowly thinned into the usual gold, and the sun struck across hills where mist curled like steam from a hundred bubbling pots. Travis relaxed in the welcome warmth, feeling his shirt dry on his shoulders. It was still a water-logged terrain ahead which should continue to slow the clan. He had high expectations of catching up with them soon, and now the worst of his bruises had faded. His muscles were limber, and he had worked out his plan as best he could.

Two hours later he sat in ambush, waiting for the scout who was walking into his hands. Under the direction of the coyotes, Travis had circled the line of march, come in ahead of the clan. Now he needed an emissary to state his challenge, and the fact that the scout he was about to jump was Manulito, one of Deklay's supporters, suited Travis' purpose perfectly. He gathered his feet under him as the other came opposite, and sprang.

The rush carried Manulito off his feet and face down on the sod while Travis made the best of his advantage and pinned the wildly fighting man under him. Had it been one of the older braves he might not have been so successful, but Manulito was still a boy by Apache standards.

"Lie still!" Travis ordered. "Listen well—so you can say to Deklay the words of the Fox!"

The frenzied struggles ceased. Manulito managed to wrench his head to the left so he could see his captor. Travis loosened his grip, got to his feet. Manulito sat up, his face darkly sullen, but he did not reach for his knife.

"You will say this to Deklay: The Fox says he is a

man of little sense and less courage, preferring to throw stones rather than meet knife to knife as does a warrior. If he thinks as a warrior, let him prove it—his strength against my strength—after the ways of the People!''

Some of the sullenness left Manulito's expression. He was eager, excited.

"You would duel with Deklay after the old custom?''

"I would. Say this to Deklay, openly so that all men may hear. Then Deklay must also give answer openly.''

Manulito flushed at that implication concerning his leader's courage, and Travis knew that he would deliver the challenge openly. To keep his hold on the clan the latter must accept it, and there would be an audience of his people to witness the success or defeat of their new chief and his policies.

As Manulito disappeared Travis summoned the coyotes, putting full effort into getting across one message. Any tribe led by Deklay would be hostile to the mutant animals. They must go into hiding, run free in the wilderness if the gamble failed Travis. Now they withdrew into the bushes but not out of reach of his mind.

He did not have too long to wait. First came Jil-Lee, Buck, Nolan, Tsoay, Lupe—those who had been with him on the northern scout. Then the others, the warriors first, the women making a half circle behind, leaving a free space in which Deklay walked.

"I am the Fox,'' Travis stated. "And this one has named me witch and *natdahe*, outlaw of the mountains. Therefore do I come to name names in my turn. Hear me, People: This Deklay—he would walk among you as *'izes-nantan*, a great chief—but he does not have the *go'ndi*, the holy power of a chief. For this Deklay is a fool, with a head filled by nothing but his own wishes, not caring for his clan brothers. He says he leads you into safety; I say he leads you into the worst danger any living man can imagine—even in peyote dreams! He is one twisted in his thoughts, and he would make you twisted also—''

Buck cut in sharply, hushing the murmur of the massed clan.

''These are bold words, Fox. Will you back them?''

Travis' hands were already peeling off his shirt. ''I will back them,'' he stated between set teeth. He had known since his awakening after the stoning that this next move was the only one left for him to make. But now that the testing of his action came, he could not be certain of the outcome, of anything save that the final decision of this battle might affect more than the fate of two men. He stripped, noting that Deklay was doing the same.

Having stepped into the center of the glade, Nolan was using the point of his knife to score a deep-ridged circle there. Naked except for his moccasins, with only his knife in his hand, Travis took the two strides which put him in the circle facing Deklay. He surveyed his opponent's finely muscled body, realizing that his earlier estimate of Deklay's probable advantages were close to the mark. In sheer strength the other outmatched him. Whether Deklay was skillful with his knife was another question, one which Travis would soon be able to answer.

They circled, eyes intent upon each move, striving to weigh and measure each other's strengths and weaknesses. Knife dueling among the Pinda-lick-o-yi, Travis remembered, had once been an art close to finished swordplay, with two evenly matched fighters able to engage for a long time without seriously marking each other. But this was a far rougher and more deadly game, with none of the niceties of such a meeting.

He evaded a vicious thrust from Deklay.

"The bull charges," he laughed. "And the Fox snaps!" By some incredible stroke of good fortune, the point of his weapon actually grazed Deklay's arm, drawing a thin, red inch-long line across the skin.

"Charge again, bull. Feel once more the Fox's teeth!"

He strode to goad Deklay into a crippling loss of temper, knowing how the other could explode into violent rage. It was dangerous, that rage, but it could also make a man blindly careless.

There was an inarticulate sound from Deklay, a dusky swelling in the man's face. He spat, as might an enraged puma, and rushed at Travis who did not quite manage to avoid the lunge, falling back with a smarting slash across the ribs.

"The bull gores!" Deklay bellowed. "Horns toss the Fox!"

He rushed again, elated by the sight of the trickling wound on Travis' side. But the slighter man slipped away.

Travis knew he must be careful in such evasions. One foot across the ridged circle and he was finished as much as if Deklay's blade had found its mark. Travis tried a thrust of his own, and his foot came down hard on a sharp pebble. Through the sole of his moccasin pain shot upward, caused him to stumble.

Again the scarlet flame of a wound, down his shoulder and forearm this time.

Well, there was one trick, he knew. Travis tossed the knife into the air, caught it with his left hand. Deklay was now facing a left-handed fighter and must adjust to that.

"Paw, bull, rattle your horns!" Travis cried. "The Fox still shows his teeth!"

Deklay recovered from his instant of surprise. With a cry which was indeed like the bellow of an old range bull, he rushed into grapple, sure of his superior strength against a younger and already wounded man.

Travis ducked, one knee thumping the ground. He groped out with his right hand, caught up a handful of earth, and flung it into the dusky brown face. Again it seemed that luck was on his side. That handful could not be as blinding as sand, but some bits of the shower landed in Deklay's eye.

For a space of seconds Deklay was wide open— open for a blow which would rip him up the middle the blow Travis could not and would not deliver.

Instead, he took the offensive recklessly, springing straight for his opponent. As the earth-grimed fingers of one hand clawed into Deklay's face, he struck with the other, not with the point of the knife but with its shaft. But Deklay, already only half conscious from the blow, had his own chance. He fell to the ground, leaving his knife behind, two inches of steel between Travis' ribs.

Somehow—he didn't know from where he drew that strength—Travis kept his feet and took one step and then another, out of the circle until the comforting brace of a tree trunk was against his bare back. Was he finished—?

He fought to nurse his rags of consciousness. Had he summoned Buck with his eyes? Or had the urgency of what he had to say reached somehow from mind to mind? The other was at his side, but Travis put out a hand to ward him off.

"Towers—" He struggled to keep his wits through the pain and billowing weakness beginning to creep through him "Reds mustn't get to the towers! Worse than the bomb . . . end us all!"

He had a hazy glimpse of Nolan and Jil-Lee closing in about him. The desire to cough tore at him, but they had to know, to believe . . .

"Reds get to the towers—everything finished. Not only here . . . maybe back home too . . ."

Did he read comprehension on Buck's face? Would Nolan and Jil-Lee and the rest believe him? Travis could not suppress the cough any longer, and the ripping pain which followed was the worst he had ever experienced. But still he kept his feet, tried to make them understand.

"Don't let them get to the towers. Find that storehouse!"

Travis stood away from the tree, reached out to Buck his earth and bloodstained hand. "I swear . . . truth . . . this must be done!"

He was going down, and he had a queer thought that once he reached the ground everything would end, not only for him but also for his mission. Trying to see the faces of the men about him was like attempting to identify the people in a dream.

"Towers!" He had meant to shout it, but he could not even hear for himself that last word as he fell.

XIV

Travis' back was braced against blanketed packs as he steadied a piece of light-yellow bark against one bent knee scowling at the lines drawn on it in faint green.

"We are here then . . . and the ship there—" His thumb was set on one point of the crude map, forefinger on the other. Buck nodded.

"That is so. Tsoay, Eskelta, Kawaykle, they watch the trails. There is the pass, two other ways men can come on foot. But who can watch the air?"

"The Tartars say the Reds dare not bring the 'copter into the mountains. After they first landed they lost a flyer in a tricky air-current flow up there. They have only one left and won't risk it. If only they aren't reinforced before we can move!" There it was again, that constant gnawing fear of time, time shortening into a rope to strangle them all.

"You think that the knowledge of our ship will bring them into the open?"

"That—or information about the towers would be the only things important enough to pull out their experts. They could send a controlled Tatar party to explore the ship, sure. But that wouldn't give them the technical reports they need. No, I think if they knew a wrecked Western Confederation ship was here, it would bring them—or enough of them to lessen the odds. We have to catch them in the open. Otherwise, they can hole up forever in that ship-fort of theirs.''

''And just how do we let them know our ship is here? Send out another scouting party and let them be trailed back?''

''That's our last resource.'' Travis continued to frown at the map. Yes, it would be possible to let the Reds sight and trail an Apache party. But there was none in the clan who were expendable. Surely there was some other way of laying the trap with the wrecked ship for bait. Capture one of the Reds, let him escape again, having seen what they wanted him to see? Again a time-wasting business. And how long would they have to wait and what risks would they take to pick up a Red prisoner?

''If the Tatars were dependable . . .'' Buck was thinking aloud.

But that ''if'' was far too big. They could not trust the Tatars. No matter how much the Mongols wanted to aid in pulling down the Reds, as long as they could be controlled by the caller they were useless. Or were they?

''Thought of something?'' Buck must have caught Travis' change of expression.

''Suppose a Tatar saw our ship and then was picked up by a Red hunting patrol and they got the information out of him?''

''Do you think any outlaw would volunteer to let himself be picked up again? And if he did, wouldn't the Reds also be able to learn that he had been set up for the trap?''

"An escaped prisoner?" Travis suggested.

Now Buck was plainly considering the possibilities of such a scheme. And Travis' own spirits rose a little. The idea was full of holes, but it could be worked out. Suppose they capture, say, Menlik, bring him here as a prisoner, let him think they were about to kill him because of the attack back in the foothills. Then let him escape, pursue him northward to a point where he could be driven into the hands of the Reds? Very chancy, but it just might work. Travis was favoring a gamble now, since his desperate one with the duel had paid off.

The risk he had accepted then had cost him two deep wounds, one of which might have been serious if Jil-Lee's project-sponsored medical training had not been to hand. But it had also made Travis one of the clan again, with his people willing to listen to his warning concerning the tower treasury.

"The girl—the Tatar girl!"

At first Travis did not understand Buck's ejaculation.

"We get the girl," the other elaborated, "let her escape, then hunt her to where they'll pick her up. Might even imprison her in the ship to begin with."

Kaydessa? Though something within him rebelled at that selection for the leading role in their drama, Travis could see the advantage of Buck's choice. Woman-stealing was an ancient pastime among primitive cultures. The Tatars themselves had found wives that way in the past, just as the Apache raiders of old had taken captive women into their wickiups. Yes, for raiders to steal a woman would be a natural act, accepted as such by the Reds. For the same woman to endeavor to escape and be hunted by her captors also was reasonable. And for such a woman, cut off from her outlaw kin, to eventually head back toward the Red settlement as the only hope of evading her enemies—logical all the way!

"She would have to be well frightened," Travis observed with reluctance.

"That can be done for us—"

Travis glanced at Buck with sharp annoyance. He would not allow certain games out of their common past to be played with Kaydessa. But Buck had something very different from old-time brutality in mind.

"Three days ago, while you were still flat on your back, Deklay and I went back to the ship—"

"Deklay?"

"You beat him openly, so he must restore his honor in his own sight. And the council has forbidden another duel or challenge," Buck replied. "Therefore he will continue to push for recognition in another way. And now that he has heard your story and knows we must face the Reds, not run from them, he is eager to take the war trial—too eager. So we returned to the ship to make another search for weapons—"

"There were none there before except those we had . . ."

"Nor now either. But we discovered something else." Buck paused and Travis was shaken out of his absorption with the problem at hand by a note in the other's voice. It was as if Buck had come upon something he could not summon the right words to describe.

"First," Buck continued, "there was this dead thing there, near where we found Dr. Ruthven. It was something like a man . . . but all silvery hair—''

''The ape-things! The ape-things from the other worlds! What else did you see?'' Travis had dropped the map. His side gave him a painful twinge as he caught at Buck's sleeve. The bald space rovers—did they still exist here somewhere? Had they come to explore the ship built on the pattern of their own but manned by Terrans?

''Nothing except tracks, a lot of them, in every open cabin and hole. I think there must have been a sizable pack of the things.''

''What killed the dead one?''

Buck wet his lips. ''I think—fear . . .'' His voice dropped a little, almost apologetically, and Travis stared.

''The ship is changed. Inside, there is something wrong. When you walk the corridors your skin crawls, you think there is something behind you. You hear things, see things from the corners of your eyes. . . . When you turn, there's nothing, nothing at all! And the higher you climb into the ship, the worse it is. I tell you, Travis, never have I felt anything like it before!''

''It was a ship of many dead,'' Travis reminded him. Had the age-old Apache fear of the dead been activated by the Redax into an acute phobia—to strike down such a level-headed man as Buck?

''No, at first that, too, was my thought. Then I discovered that it was worst not near that chamber where we lay our dead, but higher, in the Redax cabin. I think perhaps the machine is still running, but running in a wrong way—so that it does not awaken old memories of our ancestors now, but brings into being all the fears which have ever haunted us through the dark of the ages. I tell you, Travis, when I came out of that place Deklay was leading me by the hand as if I were a child. And he was shivering as a man who will never be warm again. There is an evil there beyond our understanding. I think that this Tatar girl, were she only to stay there a very short time, would be well-frightened— so frightened that any trained scientist examining her later would know there was a mystery to be explored.''

''The ape-things—could they have tried to run the Redax?'' Travis wondered. To associate machines with the creatures was outwardly pure folly. But they had been discovered on two of the planets of the old civilization, and Ashe had thought that they might represent the degenerate remnants of a once intelligent species.

''That is possible. If so, they raised a storm which drove them out and killed one of them. The ship is a haunted place now.''

''But for us to use the girl . . .'' Travis had seen the logic in Buck's first suggestion, but now he differed. If the atmosphere of the ship was as terrifying as Buck said, to imprison Kaydessa there, even temporarily, was still wrong.

''She need not remain long. Suppose we should do this: We shall enter with her and then allow the disturbance we would feel to overcome us. We could run, leave her alone. When she left the ship, we could then take up the chase, shepherding her back to the country she knows. Within the ship we would be with her and could see she did not remain too long.''

Travis could see a good prospect in that plan.

There was one thing he would insist on—if Kaydessa was to be in that ship, he himself would be one of the "captors." He said as much, and Buck accepted his determination as final.

They dispatched a scouting party to infiltrate the territory to the north, to watch and wait their chances of capture. Travis stove to regain his feet, to be ready to move when the moment came.

Five days later he was able to reach the ridge beyond which lay the wrecked ship. With him were Jil-Lee, Lupe, and Manulito. They satisfied themselves that the globe had had no visitors since Buck and Deklay; there was no sign that the ape-things had returned.

"From here," Travis said, "the ship doesn't look too bad, almost as if it might be able to take off again."

"It might lift," Jil-Lee gestured to the mountaintop behind the curve of the globe—"about that far. The tubes on this side are intact."

"What would happen were the Reds to get inside and try to fly again?" Manulito wondered aloud.

Travis was struck by a sudden idea, one perhaps just as wild as the other inspirations he had had since landing on Topaz, but one to be studied and explored—not dismissed without consideration. Suppose enough power remained to lift the ship partially and then blow it up? With the Red technicians on board at the time . . . But he was no engineer, he had no idea whether any part of the globe might or might not work again.

"They are not fools; a close look would tell them it is a wreck," Jil-Lee countered.

Travis walked on. Not too far ahead a yellow-brown shape moved out of the brush, stood stiff-legged in his path, facing the ship and growling in a harsh rumble of sound. Whatever moved or operated in that wreck was picked up by the acute sense of the coyote, even at this distance.

"On!" Travis edged around the snarling animal. With one halting step and then another, it followed him. There was a sharp warning yelp from the brush, and a second coyote head appeared. Naginlta followed Travis, but Nalik'ideyu refused to approach the grounded globe.

Travis surveyed the ship closely, trying to remember the layout of its interior. To turn the whole sphere into a trap—was it possible? How had Ashe said the Redax worked? Something about high-frequency waves stimulating certain brain and nerve centers.

What if one were shielded from those rays? That tear in the side—he himself must have climbed through that the night they crashed. And the break was not too far from the space lock. Near the lock was a storage compartment. And if it had not been jammed, or its contents crushed, they might have something. He beckoned to Jil-Lee.

"Give me a hand—up there."

"Why?"

"I want to see if the space suits are intact."

Jil-Lee regarded Travis with open bewilderment, but Manulito pushed forward. "We do not need those suits to walk here, Travis. This air we can breathe—"

"Not for the air, and not in the open." Travis advanced at a deliberate pace. "Those suits may be insulated in more ways than one—"

"Against a mixed-up Redax broadcast, you mean!" Jil-Lee exclaimed. "Yes, but you stay here, younger brother. This is a risky climb, and you are not yet strong."

Travis was forced to accede to that, waiting as Manulito and Lupe climbed up to the tear and entered. At least Buck and Deklay's experience had forewarned them and they would be prepared for the weird ghosts haunting the interior.

But when they returned, pulling between them the limp space suit, both men were pale, the shiny sheen of sweat on their foreheads, their hands shaking. Lupe sat down on the ground before Travis.

"Evil spirits," he said, giving to this modern phenomenon the old name. "Truly ghosts and witches walk in there."

Manulito had spread the suit on the ground and was examining it with a care which spoke of familiarity.

"This is unharmed," he reported. "Ready to wear."

The suits were all tailored for size, Travis knew. And this fitted a slender, medium-sized man. It would fit him, Travis Fox. But Manulito was already unbuckling the fastenings with practiced ease.

"I shall try it out," he announced. And Travis, seeing the awkward climb to the entrance of the ship, had to agree that the first test should be carried out by someone more agile at the moment.

Sealed into the suit, with the bubble helmet locked in place, the Apache climbed back into the globe. The only form of communication with him was the rope he had tied about him, and if he went above the first level, he would have to leave that behind.

In the first few moments they saw no twitch of alarm running along the rope. After counting fifty slowly, Travis gave it a tentative jerk, to find it firmly fastened within. So Manulito had tied it there and was climbing to the control cabin.

They continued to wait with what patience they could muster. Naginlta, pacing up and down a good distance from the ship, whined at intervals, the warning echoed each time by his mate upslope.

"I don't like it—" Travis broke off when the helmeted figure appeared again at the break. Moving slowly in his cumbersome clothing, Manulito reached the ground, fumbled with the catch of his head covering and then stood, taking deep, lung-filling gulps of air.

"Well?" Travis demanded.

"I see no ghosts," Manulito said, grinning. "This is ghost-proof!" He slapped his gloved hand against the covering over his chest. "There is also this—from what I know of these ships—some of the relays still work. I think this could be made into a trap. We could entice the Reds in and then . . ." His hand moved in a quick upward flip.

"But we don't know anything about the engines," Travis replied.

"No? Listen—you, Fox, are not the only one to remember useful knowledge." Manulito had lost his cheerful grin. "Do you think we are just the savages those big brains back at the project wished us to be? They have played a trick on us with their Redax. So, we can play a few tricks too. Me—? I went to M.I.T., or is that one of the things you no longer remember, Fox?"

Travis swallowed hastily. He really had forgotten that fact until this very minute. From the beginning, the Apache team had been carefully selected and screened, not only for survival potential, which was their basic value to the project, but also for certain individual skills. Just as Travis' grounding in archaelogy had been one advantage, so had Manulito's technical training made a valuable, though different, contribution. If at first the Redax, used without warning, had smothered that training, perhaps the effects were now fading.

"You can do something, then?" he asked eagerly.

"I can try. There is a chance to booby trap the control cabin at least. And that is where they would poke and pry. Working in this suit will be tough. How about my trying to smash up the Redax first?"

"Not until after we use it on our captive," Jil-Lee decided. "Then there would be some time before the Reds come—"

"You talk as if they *will* come," cut in Lupe. "How can you be sure?"

"We can't," Travis agreed. "But we can count on this much, judging from the past. Once they know that there is a wrecked ship here, they will be forced to explore it. They cannot afford an enemy settlement on this side of the mountains. That would be, according to their way of thinking, an eternal threat."

Jil-Lee nodded. "That is true. This is a complicated plan, yes, and one in which many things may go wrong. But it is also one which covers all the loopholes we know of."

With Lupe's aid Manulito crawled out of the suit. As he leaned it carefully against a supporting rock he said:

"I have been thinking of this treasure house in the towers. Suppose we could find new weapons there. . . ."

Travis hesitated. He still shrank from the thought of opening the secret places behind those glowing walls, to loose a new peril.

"If we took weapons from there and lost the fight . . ." He advanced his first objection and was glad to see the expression of comprehension on Jil-Lee's face.

"It would be putting the weapons straight into Red hands," the other agreed.

"We may have to chance it before we're through," Manulito warned. "Suppose we do get some of their technicians into this trap. That isn't going to open up their main defense for us. We may need a bigger nut-cracker than we've ever seen."

With a return of that queasy feeling he had known in the tower, Travis knew Manulito was speaking sense. They might have to open Pandora's box before the end of this campaign.

XV

THEY CAMPED another two days near the wrecked ship while Manulito prowled the haunted corridors and cabins in his space suit, planning his booby trap. At night he drew diagrams on pieces of bark and discussed the possibility of this or that device, sometimes lapsing into technicalities his companions could not follow. But Travis was well satisfied that Manulito knew what he was doing.

On the morning of the third day Nolan slipped into their midst. He was dust-grimed, his face gaunt, the signs of hard travel plain to read. Travis handed him the nearest canteen, and they watched him drink sparingly in small sips before he spoke.

"They come . . . with the girl—"

"You had trouble?" asked Jil-Lee.

"The Tatars had moved their camp, which was only wise, since the Reds must have had a line on the other one. And they are now farther to the west. But—" he wiped his lips with the back of his hand—"also we saw your towers, Fox. And that is a place of power!"

"No sign that the Reds are prowling there?"

Nolan shook his head. "To my mind the mists

there conceal the towers from aerial view. Only one coming on foot could tell them from the natural crags of the hills.''

Travis relaxed. Time still granted them a margin of grace. He glanced up to see Nolan smiling faintly.

"This maiden, she is a kin to the puma of the mountains," he announced. "She has marked Tsoay with her claws until he looks like the ear-clipped yearling fresh from the branding chute—"

"She is not hurt?" Travis demanded.

This time Nolan chuckled openly. "Hurt? No, we had much to do to keep her from hurting us, younger brother. That one is truly as she claims, a daughter of wolves. And she is also keen-witted, marking a return trail all the way, though she does not know that is as we wish. Did we not pick the easiest way back for just that reason? Yes, she plans to escape."

Travis stood up. "Let us finish this quickly!" His voice came out on a rough note. This plan had never had his full approval. Now he found it less and less easy to think about taking Kaydessa into the ship, allowing the emotional torment lurking there to work upon her. Yet he knew that the girl would not be hurt, and he had made sure he would be beside her within the globe, sharing with her the horror of the unseen.

A rattling of gravel down the narrow valley opening gave warning to those by the campfire. Manulito had already stowed the space suit in hiding. To Kaydessa they must have seemed reverted entirely to savagery.

Tsoay came first, and angry raking of four parallel scratches down his left cheek. And behind him Buck and Eskelta shoved the prisoner, urging her on with a show of roughness which did not descend to actual brutality. Her long braids had shaken loose, and a sleeve was torn, leaving one slender arm bare. But none of the fighting spirit had left her.

They thrust her out into the circle of waiting men and she planted her feet firmly apart, glaring at them all indiscriminately until she sighted Travis. Then her anger became hotter and more deadly.

"Pig! Rooter in the dirt! Diseased camel—" she shouted at him in English and then reverted to her own tongue, her voice riding up and down the scale. Her hands were tied behind her back, but there were no bonds on her tongue.

"This is one who can speak thunders, and shoot lightnings from her mouth," Buck commented in Apache. "Put her well away from the wood, lest she set it aflame."

Tsoay held his hands over his ears. "She can deafen a man when she cannot set her mark on him otherwise. Let us speedily get rid of her."

Yet for all their jeering comments, their eyes held respect. Often in the past a defiant captive who stood up boldly to his captors had received more consideration than usual from Apache warriors; courage was a quality they prized. A Pinda-lick-o-yi such as Tom Jeffords, who rode into Cochise's camp and sat in the midst of his sworn enemies for a parley, won the friendship of the very chief he had been fighting. Kaydessa had more influence with her captors than she could dream of holding.

Now it was time for Travis to play his part. He caught the girl's shoulder and pushed her before him toward the wreck.

Some of the spirit seemed to have left her thin,

tense body, and she went without any more fight. Only when they came into full view of the ship did she falter. Travis heard her breathe a gasp of surprise.

As they had planned, four of the Apaches—Jil-Lee, Tsoay, Nolan, and Buck—fanned out toward the heights about the ship. Manulito had already gone to cover, to don the space suit and prepare for any accident.

Resolutely Travis continued to propel Kaydessa ahead. At the moment he did not know which was worse, to enter the ship expecting the fear to strike, or to meet it unprepared. He was ready to refuse to enter, not to allow the girl, sullenly plodding on under his compulsion, to face that unseen but potent danger.

Only the memory of the towers and the threat of the Reds finding and exploiting the treasure there kept him going. Eskelta went first, climbing to the tear. Travis cut the ropes binding Kaydessa's wrists and gave her a slight slap between the shoulders.

"Climb, woman!" His anxiety made that a harsh order and she climbed.

Eskelta was inside now, heading for the cabin which might reasonably be selected as a prison. They planned to get the girl as far as that point and then stage their act of being overcome by fear, allowing her to escape.

Stage an act? Travis was not two feet along that corridor before he knew that there would be little acting needed on his part. The thing which pervaded the ship did not attack sharply, rather it seeped into his mind and body as if he drew in poison with every breath, sent it racing along his veins with every beat of a laboring heart. Yet he could not put any name to his feelings, except an awful weakening fear which weighted him heavier with every step he took.

Kaydessa screamed. Not this time in rage, but with such fervor that Travis lost his hold, staggered back to the wall. She whirled about, her face contorted, and sprang at him.

It was indeed like trying to fight a wildcat and after the first second or two he was hard put to protect his eyes, his face, his side, without injuring her in return. She scrambled over him, running for the break in the wall, and disappeared. Travis gasped, and started to crawl for the break. Eskelta loomed over him, pulled him up in haste.

They reached the opening but did not climb through. Travis was uncertain as to whether he could make that descent yet, and Eskelta was obeying orders in not venturing out too soon.

Below, the ground was bare. There was no sign of the Apaches, though they were in hiding there—and none of Kaydessa. Travis was amazed that she had vanished so quickly.

Still uneasy from the emanation within, they perched within the shadow of the break until Travis thought that the fugitive had a good five-minute start. Then he nodded a signal to Eskelta.

By the time they reached ground level Travis felt a warm wetness spreading under his shielding palm and he knew the wound had opened. He spoke a word or two in hot protest against that mishap, knowing it would keep him from the trail. Kaydessa must be covered all the way back across the pass, not only to be shepherded away from her people and toward the plains where she could be picked up by a Red patrol, but also to keep her from danger. And he had planned from the first to be one of those shepherds.

Now he was about as much use as a trail-lame pony. However, he could send deputies. He thought out his call, and Nalik'ideyu's head appeared in a frame of bush.

"Go, both of you and run with her! Guard—!" He said the words in a whisper, thought them with a fierce intensity as he centered his gaze on the yellow eyes in the pointed coyote face. There was a feeling of assent, and then the animal was gone. Travis sighed.

The Apache scouts were subtle and alert, but the coyotes could far outdo any man. With Nalik'ideyu and Naginlta flanking her flight, Kaydessa would be well guarded. She would probably never see her guards or know that they were running protection for her.

"That was a good move," Jil-Lee said, coming out of concealment. "But what have you done to yourself?" He stepped closer, pulling Travis' hand away from his side. By the time Lupe came to report, Travis was again wound in a strapping bandage pulled tightly about his lower ribs, and reconciled to the fact that any trailing he would do must be well to the rear of the first party.

"The towers," he said to Jil-Lee. "If our plan works, we can catch part of the Reds here. But we still have their ship to take, and for that we need help which we may find at the towers. Or at least we can be on guard there if they return with Kaydessa on that path."

Lupe dropped down lightly from an upper ledge. He was grinning.

"That woman is one who thinks. She runs from the ship first as a rabbit with a wolf at her heels. Then she begins to think. She climbs—" He lifted one finger to the slope behind them. "She goes behind a rock to watch under cover. When Fox comes from the ship with Eskelta, again she climbs. Buck lets himself be seen, so she moves east, as we wish—"

"And now?" questioned Travis.

"She is keeping to the high ways; almost she thinks like one of the People on the war trail. Nolan believes she will hole up for the night somewhere above. He will make sure."

Travis licked his lips. "She has no food or water."

Jil-Lee's lips shaped a smile. "They will see that she comes upon both as if by chance. We have planned all of this, as you know, younger brother."

That was true. Travis knew that Kaydessa would be guided without her knowledge by the "accidental" appearance now and then of some pursuer—just enough to push her along.

"Then, too, she is now armed," Jil-Lee added.

"How?" demanded Travis.

"Look to your own belt, younger brother. Where is your knife?"

Startled, Travis glanced down. His sheath was empty, and he had not needed that blade since he had drawn it to cut meat at the morning meal. Lupe laughed.

"She had steel in her hand when she came out of that ghost ship."

"Took it from me while we struggled!" Travis was openly surprised. He had considered the frenzy displayed by the Tatar girl as an outburst of almost mindless terror. Yet Kaydessa had had wit enough to take his knife! Could this be another case where one race was less affected by a mind machine than the other? Just as the Apaches had not been governed by the Red caller, so the Tatars might not be as sensitive to the Redax.

"She is a strong one, that woman—one worth many ponies." Eskelta reverted to the old measure of a wife's value.

"That is true!" Travis agreed emphatically and then was annoyed at the broadening of Jil-Lee's smile. Abruptly he changed the subject.

"Manulito is setting the booby trap in the ship."

"That is well. He and Eskelta will remain here, and you with them."

"Not so! We must go to the towers—" Travis protested.

"I thought," Jil-Lee cut in, "that you believed the weapons of the old ones too dangerous for us to use."

"Maybe they will be forced into our hands. But we must be sure the towers are not entered by the Reds on their way here."

"That is reasonable. But for you, younger brother, no trailing today, perhaps not tomorrow. If that wound opens again, you might have much bad trouble."

Travis was forced to accept that, in spite of his worry and impatience. And the next day when he did move on he had only the report that Kaydessa had sheltered beside a pool for the night and was doggedly moving back across the mountains.

Three days later, Travis, Jil-Lee, and Buck came into the tower valley. Kaydessa was in the northern foothills, twice turned back from the west and the freedom of the outlaws by the Apache scouts. And only half an hour before, Tsoay had reported by mirror what should have been welcome news: the Red helicopter was cruising as it had on the day they watched the hunters enter the uplands. There was an excellent chance of the fugitive's being sighted and picked up soon.

Tsoay had also spotted a party of three Tatars watching the helicopter. But after one wide sweep of the flyer they had taken to their ponies and ridden away at the fastest pace their mounts could manage in this rough territory.

On a stretch of smooth earth Buck scratched a trail, and studied it. The Reds would have to follow this route to seek the wrecked ship—a route covered by Apache sentinels. And following the chain of communication the result of the trap would be reported to the party at the towers.

The waiting was the most difficult; too many imponderables did not allow for unemotional thinking. Travis was down to the last shred of patience when word came on the second morning at the hidden valley that Kaydessa had been picked up by a Red patrol—drawn out to meet them by the caller.

"Now—the tower weapons!" Buck answered the report with an imperative order to Travis. And the other knew he could no longer postpone the inevitable. And only by action could he blot out the haunting mental picture of Kaydessa once more drawn into the bondage she so hated.

Flanked by Jil-Lee and Buck, he climbed back through the tower window and faced the glowing pillar.

He crossed the room, put out both hands to the sleek pole, uncertain if the weird transport would work again. He heard the sharp gasp from the others as his body was sucked against the pillar and carried downward through the well. Buck followed him, and Jil-Lee came last. Then Travis led the way along the underground corridor to the room with the table and the reader.

He sat down on the bench, fumbled with the pile of tape disks, knowing that the other two were watching him with almost hostile intentness. He snapped a disk into the reader, hoping he could correctly interpret the directions it gave.

He looked up at the wall before him. Three . . . four steps, the correct move—and then an unlocking . . .

"You know!" Buck demanded.

"I can guess—"

"Well?" Travis moved to the table. "What do we do?"

"This—" Travis came from behind the table, walked to the wall. He put out both hands, flattened his palms against the green-blue-purple surface and slid them slowly along. Under his touch, the material of the wall was cool and hard, unlike the live feel the pillar had. Cool until—

One palm, held at arm's length had found the right spot. He slid the other hand along in the opposite direction until his arms were level with his shoulders. His fingers were able now to press on those points of warmth. Travis tensed and pushed hard with all ten fingers.

XVI

AT FIRST, as one second and then two passed and there was no response to the pressure, Travis thought he had mistaken the reading of the tape. Then, directly before his eyes, a dark line cut vertically down the wall. He applied more pressure until his fingers were half numb with effort. The line widened slowly. Finally he faced a slit some eight feet in height, a little more than two in width, and there the opening remained.

Light beyond, a cold, gray gleam—like that of a cloudy winter day on Terra—and with it the chill of air out of some artic wasteland. Favoring his still bandaged side, Travis scraped through the door ahead of the others, and came into the place of gray cold.

"Wauggh!" Travis heard that exclamation from Jil-Lee, could have echoed it himself except that he was too astounded by what he had seen to say anything at all.

The light came from a grid of bars set far above their heads into the native rock which roofed this storehouse, for storehouse it was. There were orderly lines of boxes, some large enough to contain a tank, others no bigger than a man's fist. Symbols in the same blue-green-purple lights of the outer wall shone from their sides.

"What—?" Buck began one question and then changed it to another: "Where do we begin to look?"

"Toward the far end." Travis started down the center aisle between rows of the massed spoils of another time and world—or worlds. The same tape which had given him the clue to the unlocking of the door, emphasized the importance of something stored at the far end, an object or objects which must be used first. He had wondered about that tape. A sensation of urgency, almost of despair, had come through the gabble of alien words, the quick sequence of diagrams and pictures. The message might have been taped under a threat of some great peril.

There was no dust on the rows of boxes or on the floor underfoot. A current of cold, fresh air blew at intervals down the length of the huge chamber. They could not see the next aisle across the barriers of stored goods, but the only noise was a whisper and the faint sounds of their own feet. They came out into an open space backed by the wall, and Travis saw what had been so important.

"No!" His protest was involuntary, but his denial loud enough to echo.

Six—six of them—tall, narrow cases set upright against the wall; and from their depths, five pairs of dark eyes staring back at him in cold measurement. These were the men of the ships—the men Menlik had dreamed of—their bald white heads, their thin bodies with the skin-tight covering of the familiar blue-green-purple. Five of them were here, alive—watching . . . waiting . . .

Five men—and six boxes. That small fact broke the spell in which those eyes held Travis. He looked again at the sixth box to his right. Expecting to meet another pair of eyes this time, he was disconcerted to face only emptiness. Then, as his gaze traveled downward, he saw what lay on the floor there—a skull, a tangle of bones, tattered material cobwebbed into dusty rags by time. Whatever had preserved five of the star men intact, had failed the sixth of their company.

"They are alive!" Jil-Lee whispered.

"I do not think so," Buck answered. Travis took another step, reached out to touch the transparent front of the nearest coffin case. There was no change in the eyes of the alien who stood within, no indication that if the Apaches could see him, he would be able to return their interest. The five stares which had bemused the visitors at first, did not break to follow their movements.

But Travis knew! Whether it was some message on the tape which the sight of the sleepers made clear, or whether some residue of the driving purpose which had set them there now reached his mind, was immaterial. He knew the purpose of this room and its contents, why it had been made and the reason its six guardians had been left as prisoners— and what they wanted from anyone coming after them.

"They sleep," he said softly.

"They sleep in something like deep freeze."

"Do you mean they can be brought to life again!" Jil-Lee cried.

"Maybe not now—it must be too long—but they were meant to wait out a period and be restored."

"How do you know that?" Buck asked.

"I don't know for certain, but I think I understand it a little. Something happened a long time ago. Maybe it was a war, a war between whole star systems, bigger and worse than anything we can imagine. I think this planet was an outpost, and when the supply ships didn't come anymore, when they knew they might be cut off for some length of time, they closed down. Stacked their supplies and machines here and then went to sleep to wait for their rescuers. . . ."

"For rescuers who never came," Jil-Lee said softly. "And there is a chance they could be revived even now?"

Travis shivered. "Not one I would want to take."

"No," Buck's tone was somber, "that I agree to, younger brother. These are not men as we know them, and I do not think they would be good *dalaanbiyat'i*-allies. They had *go'ndi* in plenty, these star men, but it is not the power of the People. No one but a madman or a fool would try to disturb this sleep of theirs."

"The truth you speak," Jil-Lee agreed. "But where in this," he turned his shoulder to the sleeping star men and looked back at the filled chamber—"do we find anything which will serve us here and now?"

Again Travis had only the scrappiest information to draw upon. "Spread out," he told them. "Look for the marking of a circle surrounding four dots set in a diamond pattern."

They went, but Travis lingered for a moment to look once more into the bleak and bitter eyes of the star men. How many planet years ago had they sealed themselves into those boxes? A thousand, ten thousand? Their empire was long gone, yet here was an outpost still waiting to be revived to carry on its mysterious duties. It was as if in Saxon-invaded Britain long ago a Roman garrison had been frozen to await the return of the legions. Buck was right; there was no common ground today between Terran man and these unknowns. They must continue to sleep undisturbed.

Yet when Travis also turned away and went back down the aisle, he was still aware of a persistent pull on him to return. It was as though those eyes had set locking cords to will him back to release the sleepers. He was glad to turn a corner, to know that they could no longer watch him plunder their treasury.

"Here!" That was Buck's voice, but it echoed so oddly across the big chamber that Travis had difficulty in deciding what part of the warehouse it was coming from. And Buck had to call several times before Travis and Jil-Lee joined him.

There was the circle-dot-diamond symbol shining on the side of a case. They worked it out of the pile, setting it in the open. Travis knelt to run his hands along the top. The container was an unknown alloy, tough, unmarked by the years—perhaps indestructible.

Again his fingers located what his eyes could not detect—the impressions on the edge, oddly shaped impressions into which his fingertips did not fit too comfortably. He pressed, bearing down with the full strength of his arms and shoulders, and then lifted up the lid.

The Apaches looked into a set of compartments, each holding an object with a barrel, a hand grip, a general resemblance to the sidearms of their own world and time, but sufficiently different to point up the essential strangeness. With infinite care Travis worked one out of the vise-support which held it. The weapon was light in weight, lighter than any automatic he had ever held. Its barrel was long, a good eighteen inches—the grip alien in shape so that it didn't fit comfortably into his hand, the trigger nonexistent, but in its place a button on the lower part of the barrel which could be covered by an outstretched finger.

"What does it do?" asked Buck practically.

"I'm not sure. But it is important enough to have a special mention on the tape." Travis passed the weapon along to Buck and worked another loose from its holder.

"No way of loading I can see," Buck said, examining the weapon with care and caution.

"I don't think it fires a solid projectile," Travis replied. "We'll have to test them outside to find out just what we do have."

The Apaches took only three of the weapons, closing the box before they left. And as they wriggled back through the crack door, Travis was visited again by that odd flash of compelling, almost possessive power he had experienced when they had lain in ambush for the Red hunting party. He took a step or two forward until he was able to catch the edge of the reading table and steady himself against it.

"What is the matter?" Both Buck and Jil-Lee were watching him; apparently neither had felt that sensation. Travis did not reply for a second. He was free of it now. But he was sure of its source; it had not been any backlash of the Red caller! It was rooted here—a compulsion triggered to make the original intentions of the outpost obeyed, a last drag from the sleepers. This place had been set up with a single purpose: to protect and preserve the ancient rulers of Topaz. And perhaps the very presence here of the intruding Terrans had released a force, started an unseen installation.

Now Travis answered simply: "They want out. . . ."

Jil-Lee glanced back at the slit door, but Buck still watched Travis.

"They call?" he asked.

"In a way," Travis admitted. But the compulsion had already ebbed; he was free. "It is gone now."

"This is not a good place," Buck observed somberly. "We touch that which should not be held by men of our earth." He held out the weapon.

"Did not the People take up the rifles of the Pinda-lick-o-yi for their defense when it was necessary?" Jil-Lee demanded. "We do what we must. After seeing that," his chin indicated the slit and what lay behind it—"do you wish the Reds to forage here?"

"Still," Buck's words came slowly, "this is a choice between two evils, rather than between an evil and a good—"

"Then let us see how powerful this evil is!" Jil-Lee headed for the corridor leading to the pillar.

It was late afternoon when they made their way through the swirling mists of the valley under the archway giving on the former site of the outlaw Tatar camp. Travis sighted the long barrel of the weapon at a small bush backed by a boulder, and he pressed the firing button. There was no way of knowing whether the weapon was loaded except to try it.

The result of his action was quick—quick and terrifying. There was no sound, no sign of any projectile . . . ray-gas . . . or whatever might have issued in answer to his finger movement. But the bush—the bush was no more!

A black smear made a ragged outline of the extinguished ash, but the bush was gone!

"The breath of Naye'nezyani—powerful beyond belief!" Buck broke their horrified silence first. "In truth evil is here!"

Jil-Lee raised his gun—if gun it could be called—aimed at the rock with the bush silhouette plain to see and fired.

This time they were able to witness disintegration in progress, the crumble of the stone as if its substance was no more than sand lapped by river water. A pile of blackened rubble remained—nothing more.

"To use this on a living thing?" Buck protested, horror basing the doubt in his voice.

"We do not use it against living things," Travis promised, "but against the ship of the Reds—to cut that to pieces. This will open the shell of the turtle and let us at its meat."

Jil-Lee nodded. "Those are true words. But now I agree with your fears of this place, Travis. This is a devil thing and must not be allowed to fall into the hands of those who—"

"Will use it more freely than we plan to?" Buck wanted to know. "We reserve to ourselves that right because we hold our motives higher? To think that way is also a crooked trail. We will use this means because we must, but afterward . . ."

Afterward that warehouse must be closed, the

tapes giving the entrance clue destroyed. One part of Travis fought that decision, right though he knew it to be. The towers were the menace he had believed. And what was more discouraging than the risk they now ran, was the belief that the treasure was a poison which could not be destroyed but which might spread from Topaz to Terra.

Suppose the Western Conference had discovered that storehouse and explored its riches, would they have been any less eager to exploit them? As Buck had pointed out, one's own ideals could well supply reasons for violence. In the past Terra had been racked by wars of religion, one fanatically held opinion opposed to another. There was no righteousness in such struggles, only fatal ends. The Reds had no right to this new knowledge—but neither did they. It must be locked against the meddling of fools and zealots.

"Taboo—" Buck spoke that word with an emphasis they could appreciate. Knowledge must be set behind the invisible barriers of taboo, and that could work.

"These three—no more—we found no other weapons!" Jil-Lee added a warning suggestion.

"No others," Buck agreed and Travis echoed, adding:

"We found tombs of the space people, and these were left with them. Because of our great need we borrowed them, but they must be returned to the dead or trouble will follow. And they may only be used against the fortress of the Reds by us, who first found them and have taken unto ourselves the wrath of disturbed spirits."

"Well thought! That is an answer to give the

People. The towers are the tombs of dead ones. When we return these they shall be taboo. We are agreed?'' Buck asked.

"We are agreed!"

Buck tried his weapon on a sapling, saw it vanish into nothingness. None of the Apaches wanted to carry the strange guns against their bodies; the power made them objects of fear, rather than arms to delight a warrior. And when they returned to their temporary camp, they laid all three on a blanket and covered them up. But they could not cover up the memories of what had happened to bush, rock, and tree.

"If such are their small weapons," Buck observed that evening, "then what kind of things did they have to balance our heavy armament? Perhaps they were able to burn up worlds!"

"That may be what happened elsewhere," Travis replied. "We do not know what put an end to their empire. The capital-planet we found on the first voyage had not been destroyed, but it had been evacuated in haste. One building had not even been stripped of its furnishing.'' He remembered the battle he had fought there, he and Ross Murdock and the winged native, standing up to an attack of the ape-things while the winged warrior had used his physical advantage to fly above and bomb the enemies with boxes snatched from the piles. . . .

"And here they went to sleep in order to wait out some danger—time or disaster—they did not believe would be permanent," Buck mused.

Travis thought he would flee from the eyes of the sleepers throughout his dreams that night, but on the contrary he slept heavily, finding it hard to rouse when Jil-Lee awakened him for his watch. But he was alert when he saw a four-footed shape flit out of the shadows, drink water from the stream, and shake itself vigorously in a spray of drops.

"Naginlta!" he greeted the coyote. Trouble? He could have shouted that question, but he put a tight rein on his impatience and strove to communicate in the only method possible.

No, what the coyote had come to report was not trouble but the fact that the one he had been set to guard was headed back into the mountains, though others came with her—four others. Nalik'ideyu still watched their camp. Her mate had come for further orders.

Travis squatted before the animal, cupped the coyote jowls between his palms. Naginlta suffered his touch with only a small whine of uneasiness. With all his power of mental suggestion, Travis strove to reach the keen brain he knew was served by the yellow eyes looking into his.

The others with Kaydessa were to be led on, taken to the ship. But Kaydessa must not suffer harm. When they reached a spot near-by—Travis thought of a certain rock beyond the pass—then one of the coyotes was to go ahead to the ship. Let the Apaches there know . . .

Manulito and Eskelta should also be warned by the sentry along the peaks, but additional alerting would not go amiss. Those four with Kaydessa— they must reach the trap!

"What was that?" Buck rolled out of his blanket.

"Naginlta—" The coyote sped back into the dark

again. "The Reds have taken the bait, a party of at least four with Kaydessa are moving into the foot-hills, heading south."

But the enemy party was not the only one on the move. In the light of day a sentry's mirror from a point in the peaks sent another warning down to their camp.

Out in their mountain meadows the Tatar outlaws were on horseback, moving toward the entrance of the tower valley. Buck knelt by the blanket covering the alien weapons.

"Now what?"

"We'll have to stop them," Travis replied, but he had no idea of just how they would halt those deter-mined Mongol horsemen.

XVII

THERE WERE ten of them riding on small, wiry steppe ponies—men and women both, and well armed. Travis recalled it was the custom of the Horde that the women fought as warriors when necessary. Menlik—there was no mistaking the flapping robe of their leader. And they were singing! The rider behind the shaman thumped with violent energy a drum fastened beside his saddle horn, its heavy boom, boom the same call the Apache had heard before. The Mongols were working themselves into the mood for some desperate effort, Travis deduced. And if they were too deeply under the Red spell, there would be no arguing with them. He could wait no longer.

The Apache swung down from a ledge near the valley gate, moved into the open and stood waiting, the alien weapon resting across his forearm. If necessary, he intended to give a demonstration with it for an object lesson.

"Dar-u-gar!" The war cry which had once awakened fear across a quarter of Terra. Thin here, and from only a few throats, but just as menacing.

Two of the horsemen aimed lances, preparing to ride him down. Travis sighted a tree midway between them and pressed the firing button. This time there was a flash, a flicker of light, to mark the disappearance of a living thing.

One of the lancers' ponies reared, squealed in fear. The other kept on his course.

"Menlik!" Travis shouted. "Hold up your man! I do not want to kill!"

The shaman called out, but the lancer was already level with the vanished tree, his head half turned on his shoulders to witness the blackened earth where it had stood. Then he dropped his lance, sawed on the reins. A rifle bullet might not have halted his charge, unless it killed or wounded, but what he had just seen was a thing beyond his understanding.

The tribesmen sat their horses, facing Travis, watching him with the feral eyes of the wolves they claimed as forefathers, wolves that possessed the cunning of the wild, cunning enough not to rush breakneck into unknown danger.

Travis walked forward. "Menlik, I would talk—"

There was an outburst from the horsemen, protests from Hulagur and one or two of the others. But the shaman urged his mount into a walking pace toward the Apache until they stood only a few feet from each other—the warrior of the steppes and the Horde facing the warrior of the desert and the People.

"You have taken a woman from our yurts," Menlik said, but his eyes were more on the alien gun than on the man who held it. "Brave are you to come again into our land. He who sets foot in the stirrup must mount into the saddle; he who draws blade free of the scabbard must be prepared to use it."

"The Horde is not here—I see only a handful of people," Travis replied. "Does Menlik propose to go up against the Apaches so? Yet there are those who are his greater enemies."

"A stealer of women is not such a one as needs a regiment under a general to face him."

Suddenly Travis was impatient of the ceremonious talking; there was so little time.

"Listen, and listen well, Shaman!" He spoke curtly now. "I have not your woman. She is already crossing the mountains southward," he pointed with his chin—"leading the Reds into a trap."

Would Menlik believe him? There was no need, Travis decided, to tell him now that Kaydessa's part in this affair was involuntary.

"And you?" The shaman asked the question the Apache had hoped to hear.

"*We*," Travis emphasized that, "march now against those hiding behind in their ship out there." He indicated the northern plains.

Menlik raised his head, surveying the land about them with disbelieving, contemptuous appraisal.

"You are chief then of an army, an army equipped with magic to overcome machines?"

"One needs no army when he carries this." For the second time Travis displayed the power of the weapon he carried, this time cutting into shifting rubble an outcrop of cliff wall. Menlik's expression did not change, though his eyes narrowed.

The shaman signaled his small company, and they dismounted. Travis was heartened by this sign that Menlik was willing to talk. The Apache made a similar gesture, and Jil-Lee and Buck, their own weapons well in sight, came out to back him. Travis knew that the Tatar had no way of knowing that the three were alone; he well might have believed an unseen troop of Apaches were near-by and so armed.

"You would talk—then talk!" Menlik ordered.

This time Travis outlined events with an absence of word embroidery. "Kadessa leads the Reds into a trap we have set beyond the peaks—four of them ride with her. How many now remain in the ship near the settlement?"

"There are at least two in the flyer, perhaps eight more in the ship. But there is no getting at them in there."

"No?" Travis laughed softly, shifted the weapon on his arm. "Do you not think that this will crack the shell of that nut so that we can get at the meat?"

Menlik's eyes flickered to the left, to the tree which was no longer a tree but a thin deposit of ash on seared ground.

"They can control us with the caller as they did before. If we go up against them, then we are once more gathered into their net—before we reach their ship."

"That is true for you of the Horde; it does not affect the People," Travis returned. "And suppose we burn out their machines? Then will you not be free?"

"To burn up a tree? Lightning from the skies can do that."

"Can lightning," Buck asked softly, "also make rock as sand of the river?"

Menlik's eyes turned to the second example of the alien weapon's power.

"Give us proof that this will act against their machines!"

"What proof, Shaman?" asked Jil-Lee. "Shall we burn down a mountain that you may believe? This is now a matter of time."

Travis had a sudden inspiration. "You say that the 'copter is out. Suppose we use that as a target?"

"That—that can sweep the flyer from the sky?" Menlik's disbelief was open.

Travis wondered if he had gone too far. But they needed to rid themselves of that spying flyer before they dared to move out into the plain. And to use the destruction of the helicopter as an example, would be the best proof he could give of the invincibility of the new Apache arms.

"Under the right conditions," he replied stoutly, "yes."

"And those conditions?" Menlik demanded.

"That it must be brought within range. Say, below the level of a neighboring peak where a man may lie in wait to fire."

Silent Apaches faced silent Mongols, and Travis had a chance to taste what might be defeat. But the helicopter must be taken before they advanced toward the ship and the settlement.

"And, maker of traps, how do you intend to bait this one?" Menlik's question was an open challenge.

"You know these Reds better than we," Travis counterattacked. "How would you bait it, Son of the Blue Wolf?"

"You say Kaydessa is leading the Reds south; we have but your word for that," Menlick replied. "Though how it would profit you to lie on such a matter—" He shrugged. "If you do speak the truth, then the 'copter will circle about the foothills where they entered."

"And what would bring the pilot nosing farther in?" the Apache asked.

Menlik shrugged again. "Any manner of things. The Reds have never ventured too far south; they are suspicious of the heights—with good cause." His fingers, near the hilt of his tulwar, twitched. "Anything which might suggest that their party is in difficulty would bring them in for a closer look—"

"Say a fire, with much smoke?" Jil-Lee suggested.

Menlik spoke over his shoulder to his own party. There was a babble of answer, two or three of the men raising their voices above those of their companions.

"If set in the right direction, yes," the shaman conceded. "When do you plan to move, Apaches?"

"At once!"

But they did not have wings, and the cross-country march they had to make was a rough journey on foot. Travis' "at once" stretched into night hours filled with scrambling over rocks, and an early morning of preparations, with always the threat that the helicopter might not return to fly its circling mission over the scene of operations. All they had was Menlik's assurance that while any party of the Red overlords was away from their well-defended base, the flyer did just that.

"Might be relaying messages on from a walkie-talkie or something like that," Buck commented.

"They should reach our ship in two days . . . three at the most . . . if they are pushing," Travis said thoughtfully. "It would be a help—if that flyer is a link in any com unit—to destroy it before its crew picks up and relays any report of what happens back there.''

Jil-Lee grunted. He was surveying the heights above the pocket in which Menlik and two of the Mongols were piling brush. ''There . . . there . . . and there . . .'' The Apache's chin made three juts. ''If the pilot swoops for a quick look, our cross fire will take out his blades.''

They held a last conference with Menlik and then climbed to the perches Jil-Lee had selected. Sentries on lookout reported by mirror flash that Tsoay, Deklay, Lupe, and Nolan were now on the move to join the other three Apaches. If and when Manulito's trap closed its jaws on the Reds at the western ship, the news would pass and the Apaches would move out to storm the enemy fort on the prairie. And should they blast any caller the helicopter might carry, Menlik and his riders would accompany them.

There it was, just as Menlik had foretold: The wasp from the open country was flying into the hills. Menlik, on his knees, struck flint to steel, sparking the fire they hoped would draw the pilot to a closer investigation.

The brush caught, and smoke, thick and white, came first in separate puffs and then gathered into a murky pillar to form a signal no one could overlook. In Travis' hands the grip of the gun was slippery. He rested the end of the barrel on the rock, curbing his rising tension as best he could.

To escape any caller on the flyer, the Tatars had remained in the valley below the Apaches' lookout. And as the helicopter circled in, Travis sighted two men in its cockpit, one wearing a helmet identical to the one they had seen on the Red hunter days ago. The Reds' long undisputed sway over the Mongol forces would make them overconfident. Travis thought that even if they sighted one of the waiting Apaches, they would not take warning until too late.

Menlik's bush fire was performing well and the flyer was heading straight for it. The machine buzzed the smoke once, too high for the Apaches to trust raying its blades. Then the pilot came back in a lower sweep which carried him only yards above the smoldering brush, on a level with the snipers.

Travis pressed the button on the barrel, his target the fast-whirling blades. Momentum carried the helicopter on, but at least one of the marksmen, if not all three, had scored. The machine plowed through the smoke to crack up beyond.

Was their caller working, bringing in the Mongols to aid the Reds trapped in the wreck?

Travis watched Menlik make his way toward the machine, reach the cracked cover of the cockpit. But in the shaman's hand was a bare blade on which the sun glinted. The Mongol wrenched open the sprung door, thrust inward with the tulwar, and the howl of triumph he voiced was as worldless and wild as a wolf's.

More Mongols flooding down . . . Hulagur . . . a woman . . . centering on the helicopter. This time a spear plunged into the interior of the broken flyer. Payment was being extracted for long slavery.

The Apaches dropped from the heights, waiting for Menlik to leave the wild scene. Hulagur had dragged out the body of the helmeted man and the Mongols were stripping off his equipment, smashing it with rocks, still howling their war cry. But the shaman came to the dying smudge fire to meet the Apaches.

He was smiling, his upper lip raised in a curve suggesting the victory purr of a snow tiger. And he saluted with one hand.

"There are two who will not trap men again! We believe you now, *andas*, comrades of battle, when you say you can go up against their fort and make it as nothing!"

Hulagur came up behind the shaman, a modern automatic in his hand. He tossed the weapon into the air, caught it again, laughing—disclaiming something in his own language.

"From the serpents we take two fangs," Menlik translated. "These weapons may not be as dangerous as yours, but they can bite deeper, quicker, and with more force than our arrows."

It did not take the Mongols long to strip the helicopter and the Reds of what they could use, deliberately smashing all the other equipment which had survived the wreck. They had accomplished one important move: The link between the southbound exploring party and the Red headquarters—if that was the role the helicopter had played—was now gone. And the "eyes" operating over the open territory of the plains had ceased to exist. The attacking war party could move against the ship near the Red settlement, knowing they had only controlled Mongol scouts to watch for. And to penetrate enemy territory under those conditions was an old, old game the Apaches had played for centuries.

While they waited for the signals from the peaks, a camp was established and a Mongol dispatched to bring up the rest of the outlaws and all extra mounts. Menlik carried to the Apaches a portion of the dried meat which had been transported Horde fashion—under the saddle to soften it for eating.

"We do not skulk any longer like rats or city men in dark holes," he told them. "This time we ride, and we shall take an accounting from those out there—a fine accounting!"

"They still have other controllers," Travis pointed out.

"And you have that which is an answer to all their machines," blazed Menlik in return.

"They will send against us your own people if they can," Buck warned.

Menlik pulled at his upper lip. "That is also truth. But now they have no eyes in the sky, and with so many of their men away, they will not patrol too far from camp. I tell you, *andas*, with these weapons of yours a man could rule a world!"

Travis looked at him bleakly. "Which is why they are taboo!"

"Taboo?" Menlik repeated. "In what manner are these forbidden? Do you not carry them openly, use them as you wish? Are they not weapons of your own people?"

Travis shook his head. "These are the weapons of dead men—if we can name them men at all. These we took from a tomb of the star race who held Topaz when our world was only a hunting ground of wild men wearing the skins of beasts and slaying mammoths with stone spears. They are from a tomb and are cursed, a curse we took upon ourselves with their use."

There was a strange light deep in the shaman's eyes. Travis did not know who or what Menlik had been before the Red conditioner had returned him to the role of Horde shaman. He might have been a technician or scientist—and deep within him some remnants of that training could now be dismissing everything Travis said as fantastic superstition.

Yet in another way the Apache spoke the exact truth. There was a curse on these weapons, on every bit of knowledge gathered in that warehouse of the towers. As Menlik had already noted, that curse was power, the power to control Topaz, and then perhaps to reach back across the stars to Terra.

When the shaman spoke again his words were a half whisper. "It will take a powerful curse to keep these out of the hands of men."

"With the Reds gone or powerless," Buck asked, "what need will anyone have for them?"

"And if another ship comes from the skies—to begin all over again?"

"To that we shall have an answer, also, if and when we must find it," Travis replied. That could well be true . . . other weapons in the warehouse powerful enough to pluck a spaceship out of the sky, but they did not have to worry about that now.

"Arms from a tomb. Yes, this is truly dead men's magic. I shall say so to my people. When do we move out?"

"When we know whether or not the trap to the south is sprung," Buck answered.

The report came an hour after sunrise the next morning when Tsoay, Nolan, and Deklay padded into camp. The war chief made a slight gesture with one hand.

"It is done?" Travis wanted confirmation in words.

"It is done. The Pinda-lick-o-yi entered the ship

205

eagerly. Then they blew it and themselves up. Manulito did his work well."

"And Kaydessa?"

"The woman is safe. When the Reds saw the ship, they left their machine outside to hold her captive. That mechanical caller was easily destroyed. She is now free and with the *mba'a* she comes across the mountains, Manulito and Eskelta with her also. Now—" he looked from his own people to the Mongols, "why are you here with these?"

"We wait, but the waiting is over," Jil-Lee said. "Now we go north!"

XVIII

THEY LAY along the rim of a vast basin, a scooping out of earth so wide they could not sight its other side. The bed of an ancient lake, Travis speculated, or perhaps even the arm of a long-dried sea. But now the hollow was filled with rolling waves of golden grass, tossing heavy heads under the flowing touch of a breeze with the exception of a space about a mile ahead where round domes—black, gray, brown—broke the yellow in an irregular oval around the globular silver bead of a spacer: a larger ship than that which had brought the Apaches, but of the same shape.

"The horse herd . . . to the west." Nolan evaluated the scene with the eyes of an experienced raider. "Tsoay, Deklay, you take the horses!"

They nodded, and began the long crawl which would take them two miles or more from the party to stampede the horses.

To the Mongols in those domelike yurts horses were wealth, life itself. They would come running to investigate any disturbance among the grazing ponies, thus clearing the path to the ship and the Reds there. Travis, Jil-Lee, and Buck, armed with the star guns, would spearhead that attack—cutting into the substance of the ship itself until it was a sieve through which they could shake out the enemy. Only when the installations it contained were destroyed, might the Apaches hope for any assistance from the Mongols, either the outlaw pack waiting well back on the prairie or the people in the yurts.

The grass rippled and Naginlta poked out a nose, parting stems before Travis. The Apache beamed an order, sending the coyotes with the horse-raiding party. He had seen how the animals could drive hunted split-horns; they would do as well with the ponies.

Kaydessa was safe, the coyotes had made that clear by the fact that they had joined the attacking party an hour earlier. With Eskelta and Manulito she was on her way back to the north.

Travis supposed he should be well pleased that their reckless plan had succeeded as well as it had. But when he thought of the Tatar girl, all he could see was her convulsed face close to his in the ship corridor, her raking nails raised to tear his cheek. She had an excellent reason to hate him, yet he hoped . . .

They continued to watch both horse herd and domes. There were people moving about the yurts, but no signs of life at the ship. Had the Reds shut themselves in there, warned in some way of the two disasters which had whittled down their forces?

"Ah—!" Nolan breathed.

One of the ponies had raised its head and was facing the direction of the camp, suspicion plain to read in its stance. The Apaches must have reached the point between the herd and the domes which had been their goal. And the Mongol guard, who had been sitting cross-legged, the reins of his mount dangling close to his hand, got to his feet.

"Ahhhuuuuu!" The ancient Apache war cry that had sounded across deserts, canyons, and southwestern Terran plains to ice the blood, ripped just as freezingly through the honey-hued air of Topaz.

The horses wheeled, racing upslope away from the settlement. A figure broke from the grass, flapped his arms at one of the mounts, grabbed at flying mane, and pulled himself up on the bare back. Only a master horseman would have done that, but the whooping rider now drove the herd on, assisted by the snapping and snarling coyotes.

"Deklay—" Jil-Lee identified the reckless rider, "that was one of his rodeo tricks."

Among the yurts it was as if someone had ripped up a rotten log to reveal an ants' nest and sent the alarmed insects into a frenzy. Men boiled out of the domes, the majority of them running for the horse pasture. One or two were mounted on ponies that must have been staked out in the settlement. The main war party of Apaches skimmed silently through the grass on their way to the ship.

The three who were armed with the alien weapons had already tested their range by experimentation back in the hills, but the fear of exhausting whatever powered those barrels had curtailed their target practice. Now they snaked to the edge of the bare ground between them and the ladder hatch of the spacer. To cross that open space was to provide targets for lances and arrows—or the superior armament of the Reds.

"A chance we can hit from here." Buck laid his weapon across his bent knee, steadied the long barrel of the burner, and pressed the firing button.

The closed hatch of the ship shimmered, dissolved

into a black hole. Behind Travis someone let out the yammer of a war whoop.

"Fire—cut the walls to pieces!"

Travis did not need that order from Jil-Lee. He was already beaming unseen destruction at the best target he could ask for—the side of the sphere. If the globe was armed, there was no weapon which could be depressed far enough to reach the marksmen at ground level.

Holes appeared, irregular gaps and tears in the fabric of the ship. The Apaches were turning the side of the globe into lacework. How far those rays penetrated into the interior they could not guess.

Movement at one of the holes, the chattering burst of machine-gun fire, spatters of soil and gravel into their faces; they could be cut to pieces by that! The hole enlarged, a scream . . . cut off . . .

"They will not be too quick to try that again," Nolan observed with cold calm from behind Travis' post.

Methodically they continued to beam the ship. It would never be space-borne again; there were neither the skills nor materials here to repair such damage.

"It is like laying a knife to fat," Lupe said as he crawled up beside Travis. "Slice, slice—!"

"Move!" Travis reached to the left, pulled at Jil-Lee's shoulder.

Travis did not know whether it was possible or not, but he had a heady vision of their combined fire power cutting the globe in half, slicing it crosswise with the ease Lupe admired.

They scurried through cover just as someone behind yelled a warning. Travis threw himself down, rolled into a new firing position. An arrow sang over his head; the Reds were doing what the Apaches had known they would—calling in the controlled Mongols to fight. The attack on the ship must be stepped up, or the Amerindians would be forced to retreat.

Already a new lacing of holes appeared under their concentrated efforts. With the gun held tight to his middle, Travis found his feet, zigzagged across the bare ground for the nearest of those openings. Another arrow clanged harmlessly against the fabric of the ship a foot from his goal.

He made it in, over jagged metal shards which glowed faintly and reeked of ozone. The weapons' beams had penetrated well past both the outer shell and the wall of insulation webbing. He climbed a second and smaller break into a corridor enough like those of the western ship to be familiar. The Red spacer, based on the general plan of the alien derelict ship as his own had been, could not be very different.

Travis tried to subdue his heavy breathing and listen. He heard a confused shouting and the burr of what might be an alarm system. The ship's brain was the control cabin. Even if the Reds dared not try to lift now, that was the core of their communication lines. He started along the corridor, trying to figure out its orientation in relation to that all-important nerve center.

The Apache shoved open each door he passed with one shoulder, and twice he played a light beam on installations within cabins. He had no idea of their use, but the wholesale destruction of each and every machine was what good sense and logic dictated.

There was a sound behind. Travis whirled, saw Jil-Lee and beyond him Buck.

"Up?" Jil-Lee asked.

"And down," Buck added. "The Tatars say they have hollowed a bunker beneath."

"Separate and do as much damage as you can," Travis suggested.

"Agreed!"

Travis sped on. He passed another door and then backtracked hurriedly as he realized it had given on to an engine room. With the gun he blasted two long lines cutting the fittings into ragged lumps. Abruptly the lights went out; the burr of the alarms was silenced. Part of the ship, if not all, was dead. And now it might come to hunter and hunted in the dark. But that was an advantage as far as the Apaches were concerned.

Back in the corridor again, Travis crept through a curiously lifeless atmosphere. The shouting was stilled as if the sudden failure of the machines had stunned the Reds.

A tiny sound—perhaps the scrape of a boot on a ladder. Travis edged back into a compartment. A flash of light momentarily lighted the corridor; the approaching figure was using a torch. Travis drew his knife with one hand, reversed it so he could use the heavy hilt as a silencer. The other was hurrying now, on his way to investigare the burned-out engine cabin. Travis could hear the rasp of his fast breathing. Now!

The Apache had put down the gun, his left arm closed about a shoulder, and the Red gasped as Travis struck with the knife hilt. Not clean—he had to hit a second time before the struggles of the man were over. Then, using his hands for eyes, he stripped the limp body on the floor of automatic and torch.

With the Red's weapon in the front of his sash, the burner in one hand and the torch in the other, Travis prowled on. There was a good chance that those above might believe him to be their comrade returning. He found the ladder leading to the next level, began to climb, pausing now and then to listen.

Shock preceded sound. Under him the ladder swayed and the globe itself rocked a little. A blast of some kind must have been set off at or under the level of the ground. The bunker Buck had mentioned?

Travis clung to the ladder, waited for the vibrations to subside. There was a shouting above, a questioning. . . . Hurriedly he ascended to the next level, scrambled out and away from the ladder just in time to avoid the light from another torch flashed down the well. Again that call of inquiry, then a shot—the boom of the explosion loud in the confined space.

To climb into the face of that light with a waiting marksman above was sheer folly. Could there be another way up? Travis retreated down one of the corridors raying out from the ladder well. A quick inspection of the cabins along that route told him he had reached a section of living quarters. The pattern was familiar; the control cabin would be on the next level.

Suddenly the Apache remembered something: On each level there should be an emergency opening giving access to the insulation space between the inner and outer skins of the ship through which repairs could be made. If he could find that and climb up to the next level . . .

The light shining down the well remained steady, and there was the echoing crack of another shot. But Travis was far enough away from the ladder now to dare use his own torch, seeking the door he needed on the wall surface. With a leap of heart he sighted the outline—his luck was in! The Russian and western ships were alike.

Once the panel was open he flashed his torch up, finding the climbing rungs and, above, the shadow outline of the next level opening. Securing the alien gun in his sash beside the automatic and holding the torch in his mouth, Travis climbed, not daring to think of the deep drop below. Four . . . five . . . ten rungs, and he could reach the other door.

His fingers slid over it, searching for the release catch. But there was no answering give. Balling his fist, he struck down at an awkward angle and almost lost his balance as the panel fell away beneath his blow. The door swung and he pulled through.

Darkness! Travis snapped on the torch for an instant, saw about him the relays of a com system, and gave it a full spraying as he pivoted, destroying the eyes and ears of the ship—unless the burnout he had effected below had already done that. A flash of automatic fire from his left, a searing burn along his arm an inch or so below the shoulder—

Travis' action was purely reflex. He swung the burner around, even as his mind gave a frantic No! To defend himself with automatic, knife, arrow—yes; but not this way. He huddled against the wall.

An instant earlier there had been a man there, a living, breathing man—one of his own species, if not of his own beliefs. Then because his own muscles had unconsciously obeyed warrior training, there was this. So easy—to deal death without really meaning to. The weapon in his hands was truly the devil gift they were right to fear. Such weapons were not to be put into the hands of men—any men—no matter how well intentioned.

Travis gulped in great mouthfuls of air. He wanted to throw the burner away, hurl it from him. But the task he could rightfully use it for was not yet done.

Somehow he reeled on into the control cabin to render the ship truly a dead thing and free himself of the heavy burden of guilt and terror between his hands. That weight could be laid aside; memory could not. And no one of his kind must ever have to carry such memories again.

The booming of the drums was like a pulse quickening the blood to a rhythm which bit at the brain, made a man's eyes shine, his muscles tense as if he held an arrow to bow cord or arched his fingers about a knife hilt. A fire blazed high and in its light men leaped and whirled in a mad dance with tulwar blades catching and reflecting the red gleam of flames. Mad, wild, the Mongols were drunk with victory and freedom. Beyond them, the silver globe of the ship showed the black holes of its death, which was also the death of the past—for all of them.

"What now?" Menlik, the dangling of amulets and charms tingling as he moved, came up to Travis. There was none of the wild fervor in the shaman's face; instead, it was as if he had taken several strides out of the life of the Horde, was emerging into another person, and the question he asked was one they all shared.

Travis felt drained, flattened. They had achieved their purpose. The handful of Red overlords were dead, their machines burned out. There were no controls here any more; men were free in mind and body. What were they to do with that freedom?

"First," the Apache spoke his own thoughts —"we must return these."

The three alien weapons were lashed into a square of Mongol fabric, hidden from sight, although they could not be so easily shut out of mind. Only a few of the others, Apache or Mongol, had seen them; and they must be returned before their power was generally known.

"I wonder if in days to come," Buck mused, "they will not say that we pulled lightning out of the sky, as did the Thunder Slayer, to aid us. But this is right. We must return them and make that valley and what it holds taboo."

"And what if another ship comes—one of *yours?*" Menlik asked shrewdly.

Travis stared beyond the Tatar shaman to the men about the fire. His nightmare dragged into the open . . . What if a ship did come in, one with Ashe, Murdock, men he knew and liked, friends on board? What then of his guardianship of the towers and their knowledge? Could he be as sure of what to do then? He rubbed his hand across his forehead and said slowly:

"We shall take steps when—or if—that happens—"

But could they, would they? He began to hope fiercely that it would not happen, at least in his lifetime, and then felt the cold bleakness of the exile they must will themselves into.

"Whether we like it or not," (was he talking to the others or trying to argue down his own rebellion?) "we cannot let what lies under the towers be known . . . found . . . used . . . unless by men who are wiser and more controlled than we are in our time."

Menlik drew his shaman's wand, twiddled it between his fingers, and beneath his drooping lids watched the three Apaches with a new kind of measurement.

"Then I say to you this: Such a guardianship must be a double charge, shared by my people as well. For if they suspect that you alone control these powers and their secret, there will be envy, hatred, fear, a division between us from the first—war . . . raids . . . This is a large land and neither of our groups numbers many. Shall we split apart fatally from this day when there is room for all? If these ancient things are evil, then let us both guard them with a common taboo."

He was right, of course. And they would have to face the truth squarely. To both Apache and Mongol any off-world ship, no matter from which side, would be a menace. Here was where they would remain and set roots. The sooner they began thinking of themselves as people with a common bond, the better it would be. And Menlik's suggestion provided a tie.

"You speak well," Buck was saying. "This shall be a thing we share. We are three who know. Do you be three also, but choose well, Menlik!"

"Be assured that I will!" the Tatar returned. "We start a new life here; there is no going back. But as I have said: The land is wide. We have no quarrel with one another, and perhaps our two peoples shall become one; after all, we do not differ too greatly. . . ." He smiled and gestured to the fire and the dancers.

Among the Mongols another man had gone into action, his head thrown back as he leaped and twirled, voicing a deep war cry. Travis recognized Deklay. Apache, Mongol—both raiders, horsemen, hunters, fighters when the need arose. No, there was no great difference. Both had been tricked into coming here, and they had no allegiance now for those who had sent them.

Perhaps clan and Horde would combine or perhaps they would drift apart—time would tell. But there would be the bond of the guardianship, the determination that what slept in the towers would not be roused—in their lifetime or many lifetimes!

Travis smiled a bit crookedly. A new religion of sorts, a priesthood with sacred and forbidden knowledge . . . in time a whole new life and civilization stemming from this night. The bleak cold of his early thought cut less deep. There was a different kind of adventure here.

He reached out and gathered up the bundle of the burners, glancing from Buck to Jil-Lee to Menlik. Then he stood up, the weight of the burden in his arms, the feeling of a greater weight inside him.

"Shall we go?"

To get the weapons back—that was of first importance. Maybe then he could sleep soundly, to dream of riding across the Arizona range at dawn under a blue sky with a wind in his face, a wind carrying the scent of piñon pine and sage, a wind which would never caress or hearten him again, a wind his sons and sons' sons would never know. To dream troubled dreams, and hope in time those dreams would fade and thin—that a new world would blanket out the old. Better so, Travis told himself with defiance and determination—better so!